46 858 432 X

———

Please rene.
shown on your .

www.hertsdirect.c. ₃

Renewals and enquiries:

Textpho~~ for hearing or   0₃₆
speech

L32

Hert.

"Things are never going to be strictly business between us, Gabi.

The past is always going to be there along with that one question."

Don't ask.

Don't do it.

"What question?"

Kingsley leaned in even closer, and she had to fight the urge to bolt away from him. But she wouldn't let him know he was getting to her. She had to stand firm. He was just a man.

No.

He was more than a man. He was her own personal demon. One that she hadn't exorcised because she'd never been able to see him as anything other than a hot fantasy. They'd barely dated before they'd slept together, and then everything had fallen apart.

She couldn't let him continue to dominate every moment they had together.

"If that one night together was a fluke," he said.

He leaned in closer. So close that she'd barely have to incline her head for their lips to brush.

His Baby Agenda

KATHERINE
GARBERA

First published in Great Britain 2016
By Mills & Boon, an imprint of HarperCollins*Publishers*
1 London Bridge Street, London, SE1 9GF

Large Print edition 2016

© 2016 Katherine Garbera

ISBN: 978-0-263-06632-6

Our policy is to use papers that are natural, renewable and recyclable products and made from wood grown in sustainable forests. The logging and manufacturing processes conform to the legal environmental regulations of the country of origin.

Printed and bound in Great Britain
by CPI Antony Rowe, Chippenham, Wiltshire

USA TODAY bestselling author **Katherine Garbera** is a two-time MAGGIE® Award winner who has written more than seventy books. A Florida native who grew up to travel the globe, Katherine now makes her home in the Midlands of the UK with her husband, two children and a very spoiled miniature dachshund. Visit Katherine on the web at katherinegarbera.com, or catch up with her on Facebook and Twitter.

This book is dedicated to Courtney and Lucas. No mother could be prouder of her children than I am of you.

Thank you to my wonderful editor, Charles, for his insights and knowing the right questions to ask in order to make my manuscripts better. Thank you also to my dear friend Eve Gaddy, who is always available to chat about my plot when I run into problems.

One

The intercom buzzed and Gabriella de la Cruz put down her cup of tea to pick up the phone. "Yes, Melissa?"

"There is someone here to see you," her assistant said. To Gabi's ears Melissa sounded excited, the way she'd been that time she'd won five hundred dollars on a scratch-off lottery card. She could only guess that another one of the celebrities Melissa was always cyberstalking had dropped by looking for a nanny.

Gabi had started her nanny service seven years ago after a very successful run as a live-in nanny for the Hollywood director Malcolm Jeffers. Mal and his wife had sung Gabi's praises and suggested she start her own business when their kids were old enough to no longer need a nanny.

"I have an appointment in thirty minutes," Gabi said. "Can you ask them to come back?"

"I think you'll want to see *him*," Melissa said.

Doubtful. She was busy; it seemed as though everyone wanted something from her at this time of year. Her parents wanted her to make more time for them and come over to their place this weekend. Her clients were anxious about summer and instead of dealing with the nannies who worked in their homes year-round, they were calling her about activities, vacations and travel documents. Her clientele couldn't just nip down to Disneyland or Legoland for the weekend. They all wanted to go someplace exotic, which was a big headache.

"Who is it?" she asked at last. Melissa wasn't going to just tell him to go away. And Gabi needed to get back to writing the column she was working on for a national parenting magazine.

"It's Kingsley Buchanan. The former NFL

quarterback, agent to the best athletes in the world."

Kingsley.

Of course when she was having a bad day he'd have to walk back into her life. Heck, even just his name sent a shiver through her. She wanted to pretend it was one of dread, but her pulse had picked up and she'd sat up a little straighter.

"I don't have the time," she said, hanging up the phone.

Let's face it; she didn't owe him more than that. He'd been her first lover—well, one-night stand might be more accurate given that he'd left her in the morning and been arrested before lunch. She'd only been alone with him one time after that. An ill-fated jailhouse visit when he'd told her she'd been naive to think there was more between them than what she'd gotten.

Idiot.

She wasn't sure if she meant him or herself.

Why was he here?

Why did she care?

She reached up to push her hair behind her ear and then pulled her laptop closer, staring at the screen and pretending she was reading the email her mother had sent about the first communion of her cousin Guillermo's daughter in Spain this summer. But she wasn't.

Why was Kingsley here?

Her door opened without a knock and she glanced up to see broad shoulders filling the doorway. She caught her breath. Of course she'd seen him on television in the past ten years—just occasionally—before she quickly changed the channel. But damn, time had been good to him.

His thick dark brown hair, longer on the top, was artfully styled; it must have had some sort of product in it to keep it in place. His eyes were still blue, but in her mind they seemed icier than they had been in college. His jaw was hard, square and stubbornly set, his beard neatly trimmed.

"Can I help you?"

"That's why I'm here," he said, walking into the room as if he owned it, closing the door behind him.

"I believe I asked Melissa to schedule you an

appointment for later in the week. I'm booked solid."

"Surely you can make time for an old friend," he said.

But there was nothing friendly in his manner as he walked over to her desk and perched his hip on the edge of it. He did casual the way a tiger hunting its prey did it. She tried to convince herself she bore no resemblance to a mouse as she looked up at him.

Take control.

That was what she'd learned after years of dealing with recalcitrant parents and children.

She stood up and held her hand out to him. Time to put this on a business footing. She'd shake his hand and walk him back to the door and then gently tell him goodbye.

Solid plan.

She was a genius.

"It's wonderful to see you again, Kingsley. But I'm afraid I really don't have time this morning."

He took her hand in his but didn't shake it. He held it loosely, stroking his thumb over her knuckles and making goose bumps spread up

her arm. His amused look as she pulled her hand
free made her want to do something to jar him.

But she wasn't young and impulsive. He'd been
the one to show her that being impetuous was
the path to disaster. She stepped away from him.

"Why are you here?" she asked at last. "I think
we've said all that needed to be said."

"I'm looking for a nanny," he said.

"I'm afraid my business only caters to real
children, not those stuck in men's bodies."

He gave a bark of laughter and shook his head.
"I'd forgotten that there was always a little edge
to you."

He had no idea.

"You don't know me," she said carefully. "And
really, I can see we have nothing further to discuss, so if you wouldn't mind leaving."

"But I would mind," he said. "I'm not one of
your naughty clients who you can *firmly control
with your calm tones.*"

She tipped her head to the side to study him.
How did he know about her techniques? She'd
written those very words last month in her column. Why was he here?

"For the last time, Kingsley, why are you here?"

"I told you, Gabriella, I need you."

The way he said her name, letting it roll off his tongue as his tone deepened, weakened her resolve to get him out of her office quickly. And he'd said he needed her...the words she'd been waiting ten years to hear.

"Too bad. I don't want to give the impression of being a clingy woman who doesn't know when a lover has had enough."

Kingsley had known coming back to California would be difficult, but he'd never shied away from obstacles. Experience had taught him that anything that didn't kill him made him stronger. He knew it was a cliché, but a decade ago he'd spent a rough six months being treated as a murderer before being cleared of charges. Rumors had swirled that his father had bought off the grand jury, but in the end there was no evidence and they'd had to let both him and the other suspect—his best friend, Hunter Carruthers—go. But that reputation had followed him into the

NFL and he'd always been considered dangerous by his teammates and a publicity liability
by his coaches and managers.

Over the years he'd learned to bury his emotions, beneath a layer of ice so that no one could
rattle him. But all that seemed to be out the window now that he was in the same room as Gabi
de la Cruz once again.

She'd grown into her beauty. Her caramel-colored hair was thick and long, falling past her
shoulders in smooth waves. Her eyes were still
deep brown, but instead of revealing every emotion she felt, they were cautious. She watched
him warily—something he knew he deserved—
as if he were about to pounce on her.

He'd be lying if he said she didn't still turn
him on.

She'd always been different from other women,
which was why he'd been quick to distance himself from her after Stacia Krushnik had been
found dead. But that was the past. A past that really didn't concern Gabi, thanks to the heartless
way he'd sent her from his life. He was back in
California for revenge and he needed someone

to keep his son protected from the shit storm that he suspected he and Hunter Carruthers were about to unleash.

"I'm not here for a lover, Gabi. I'm here because I need a nanny for my son."

"Your son?" she asked.

"Yes," he said. He'd followed her through the years via newspaper articles and online social media; it was a hit to his ego that she hadn't done the same. "Conner is three and desperately in need of a nanny."

He'd confused her.

Good. Finally, he felt as though the advantage was swinging back toward him.

She brushed past him; the subtle scent of her flowery perfume surrounded him as she sat down behind her desk. She reached for a piece of monogrammed paper and drew it toward her.

"Conner is three?" she asked. "What kind of nanny are you looking for?"

"You. I have spoken to Mal and he said you were the best. And I've read your parenting articles—I like your theories on child rearing."

"Thank you," she said, bowing her head

slightly. "Why don't you have a seat while we discuss this?"

"I'm comfortable here," he said.

She gave him a tight smile. He bit the inside of his mouth to keep from smiling back. He was unnerving her. He liked it.

"Will your wife be part of the interview process for the nanny?" Gabi asked.

"She's dead."

"Oh," she said, looking up at him. "I'm sorry, Kingsley."

"It's okay," he said. "Conner doesn't remember her at all. It happened when he was six months old."

"What have you been doing for child care up to now?" she asked.

He'd been using his assistant, Peri, but she'd gotten married last month and was retiring. "My assistant. How soon can you start?"

"I can't."

"What?"

"I don't nanny anymore. I have a couple of nannies that are coming off assignments in the next week or so. I can set up some interviews for you, and I'd like to meet your son myself. Where is he?"

"With Hunter," Kingsley said. Hunter and he had been a great duo on the field in college, and after Stacia's death, Hunter had stopped playing football, being the second son of a privileged family. Hunter hadn't needed to work, so he had spent the past few years building his reputation as a playboy. Plus the stigma of being charged with the "Frat House Murder" hadn't helped.

"Um…we need to talk about that. He's got a wild reputation. I can't place one of my nannies in your home if he's going to be there."

"He won't be a problem," Kingsley said. "I don't want one of your nannies. I want you, Gabi."

"I can't."

"Why not?"

"I'm not in the field anymore."

"I'll make it worth your while," he said. If there was one thing he'd learned from his father, Jeb Buchanan, it was that everyone had a price. Many people believed his father had bought Kingsley's freedom and the silence of witnesses. But Jeb had a strong sense of justice and no one, not even his wayward younger son, could escape that. His father still wasn't convinced that Kingsley was innocent in Stacia's death.

But after Kingsley was done with his revenge, there would be no doubt as to who was responsible for her death.

"I can't be bought."

"No? What if I offered to fund the new playground you have been trying to get built?" he asked.

Gabi wouldn't do it for herself, but he remembered her soft heart and how she'd do anything for a good cause. He wondered if that had changed.

She chewed her lower lip and looked down at the paper in front of her.

It hadn't.

His gut was still right on the money when it came to this woman.

"We are talking a six-figure sum, Kingsley. Is my being a nanny to Conner worth that much?"

It was. He needed her to watch over his son

and he needed her recollections of that party the night Stacia had died. Once he had her living under his roof, he'd be able to get the answers he needed.

There were certain parts of the night that didn't add up. And everyone he and Hunter had spoken to had a different version of the events. So whether it took six figures or nine, it didn't matter. He needed to put the ghosts of the past to rest. And Gabi was the only woman who could help him do that.

"Yes," he said. "I'll need you in my home by this evening. I've left my address with your assistant."

"I've agreed to be Conner's nanny, but that's it. I'm not living in," she said.

"For the amount I'm paying, I think you are," he said.

He stood up and starting walking to the door. He'd accomplished what he'd set out to do. It was time to get back to the rest of his day.

Arrogant bastard.

Gabi got up from her desk and dashed around

in front of Kingsley before he could get to the door. She pressed her back against it and gave him a hard look.

She knew it was important to establish right this moment that he wasn't in charge. No matter how much it might seem otherwise.

"We're not finished yet."

"I can't imagine what else we have to discuss," he said.

He didn't stop as she'd thought he would. Instead he came right up until barely an inch of space separated them and put his hands on the door on either side of her head.

He surrounded her. She could see the flecks of green in his icy-blue eyes and the scar on his left eyebrow that she'd noticed the first time he'd kissed her. Her lips felt dry. Her breath got shallower and she wanted to smack herself in the forehead. *Don't react to him.*

This was Kingsley Buchanan—lover and leaver. Not a man she was interested in.

But her body said otherwise.

Every nerve inside her reacted to him as if she didn't know he was bad news. As if she hadn't just agreed to live in his house... It was a deal with the devil.

Sure, she'd been battling with the county commissioners for the last eighteen months trying to get that park and playground built. And Kingsley's offer was too good to pass up. But he didn't own her. She had to stay in control.

Except his cologne smelled so good.

"We have a lot to discuss," she said. Her voice sounded thready and breathy to her own ears.

Ugh.

"Like what?"

"I'm not living in your house."

"Nonnegotiable."

She frowned at him.

"Everything is."

"Not that. I travel a lot with my job and I work from my home office. I need 24-7 care for Conner."

"I can't work 24-7 for you. I have to run this business," she said.

"I will give you an office in my home and if your office hours are flexible, I'm willing to work with your schedule to give you the time you need. But you must live in my house."

No, she thought. She couldn't do it. But there was something persuasive about him and she felt her resolve weakening. He was a client; she'd keep it all business.

"Okay. We can try it out. But if I feel like it's not working, then we will have to figure out something else."

"I'm sure it will work."

Of course he was.

"Was that all?" he asked.

All?

He leaned in closer and she felt the brush of his breath over her mouth. Her lips parted and she realized that she was never going to be all business with him. There was no way.

"No."

"No?"

"I need some resolution to the past," she said. "You can't be this close to me."

"You're the one blocking the door with your body."

She narrowed her eyes at him. He had a point,

but he was still crowding her and he had been since he came into her office. "I mean it. Our arrangement is strictly business."

His left hand shifted on the door and she felt his fingers in her hair. Her scalp tingled and sensation spread slowly downward. "Things are never going to be strictly business between us, Gabi. The past is always going to be there along with that one question."

Don't ask.

Don't do it.

"What question?"

He leaned in even closer and she had to fight the urge to bolt away from him. But she wouldn't let him know he was getting to her. She had to stand firm. He was just a man.

No.

He was more than a man. He was her own personal demon. One that she hadn't exorcised because she'd never been able to see him as anything other than a hot fantasy. They'd barely dated before they'd slept together and then everything had fallen apart.

She couldn't let him continue to dominate every moment they had together.

"If that one night together was a fluke," he said.

He leaned in closer. So close that she'd barely have to incline her head for their lips to brush. Sure, she remembered their night together, but it had become hazy over the years, tinged with regret and anger. She wanted to take back something that she hadn't realized Kingsley had stolen until this moment, a part of her womanhood that he'd damaged when he'd left her.

She put her hands on his shoulders and went up on tiptoe, so they were eye to eye. He was impossible to read. He'd always been hard, but now there was a new layer of ice in his gaze. A new barrier that she couldn't see past.

For her own sanity, she had to keep this strictly business. She was twenty-eight and finally felt that she was getting her life on track. She wouldn't let a man like Kingsley derail that.

"Oh, I thought you meant if I'd still want you," she said, trying to turn the tables on him.

"Do you?"

She dashed to the side, ducking out from under his arm. "I've sort of outgrown bad boys."

"Have you?"

"All girls do when they grow up," she said. "Melissa will send over a contract. Good day, Kingsley."

Two

Kingsley wasn't sure if he'd won or lost the battle with Gabi. She'd always had the unique ability to throw him. Even in college before… everything had gone crazy, she'd rattled him. But the past ten years had changed him. And though he'd enjoyed flirting with her—hell, he was a red-blooded male, of course he enjoyed flirting with her—that wasn't why he was back in California, and he had to stay focused.

He got in his Porsche 911, driving a little over the speed limit as he headed to his new home. The mansion he'd purchased was perched on a cliff above the Pacific with a path to the beach that he intended to use frequently with his son. He'd been working hard—well, running from his past was more like it—since he'd left California. Now he was back and he knew one thing: he couldn't raise his son in a world where he had had to face that kind of stigma.

It was one thing that Stacia's death had left Kingsley mired in scandal. But he wouldn't let it touch Conner.

His phone rang, blasting out "Bad to the Bone." He hit the answer button on his hands free.

"What's up, Hunter? Is Conner okay?"

"He's fine, the little devil. I'm worn-out. I think he's got the makings of a running back," Hunter said. "Did she agree?"

Hunter wasn't the playboy the media made him out to be. Kingsley knew they'd still be best friends even if they hadn't been linked together in Stacia's murder. He was closer to Hunter than he was to his own brother.

"Yes, she did. I didn't mention anything about Stacia. I want to get Gabi out to my house so I can be subtle about the questioning," he said.

"Hey, it's your plan. I'm happy enough to let

you set the pace. I just want to get some answers," Hunter said.

Hunter could barely remember the entire night.
And that was a little worrying, since his friend
hadn't been a big drinker in college. One the-
ory they had was that someone had put a drug
in Stacia's drink—she and Hunter had been dating—and that Hunter had ingested some of it
over the course of the night.

"When will you be home? I've got a meeting
with Tristan Sabine in forty-five minutes."

"I'll be there in twenty," Kingsley said. Tristan
was one of the founders of a chain of nightclubs
called Seconds. In fact, Gabi's cousin Gui was
another owner. Hunter had recently purchased a
franchise of the club and opened it in San Fran-
cisco, to much success.

"Sounds great," Hunter said. "I'm glad we're
back here. It's way past time we got some answers and gave Stacia's ghost some peace."

And themselves, Kingsley thought. They'd
never been able to live with Stacia's murder or
the fact that it had never really been solved.

He disconnected the call and concentrated on

the traffic, but his mind wasn't really on the past or the drive. Gabi dominated his thoughts the same as she had back in college.

She'd changed.

Really, idiot?

But that was the best he could do. She had changed. It wasn't just maturing—it was more than that. There was a level of confidence that hadn't been in her at eighteen. A level of self-assurance that enabled her to stand her ground with him.

He admired that.

He wished…hell, there wasn't a day that had gone by in the past ten years that he hadn't regretted what he'd said when she'd come to see him in jail. Regretted it only insomuch as he knew he'd hurt her. He didn't regret that he'd gotten her out of the jailhouse before the press had descended. He'd kept her safe from the scandal that had rained down around him and Hunter.

But now…

The woman she was today could handle things that the girl she'd been hadn't been able to. That didn't mean he still wouldn't protect her. He had to get his revenge and keep Conner and Gabi from being hit with the fallout. That was going to take all of the skills he'd learned on and off the football field. Things such as faking out the rushers, keeping the press from seeing past his smile and definitely winning.

He pulled to a stop in the big circle drive in front of his house. The front door opened just as he shut off his car and stepped out of it.

Conner came running down the steps, laughing.

"Daddy!"

Kingsley scooped up his son and kissed the top of his head. Conner had Kingsley's own blue eyes, but Jade's reddish-blond hair.

"Get back here, imp," Hunter said, skidding to a halt in the doorway.

"Um, why was my son running outside?" Kingsley asked.

"'Cause he's spoiled," Hunter said.

"I am," Conner said.

Kingsley was pretty sure that Conner had no idea what spoiled meant, but he and Hunter were very close and Conner almost always agreed with his favorite "uncle."

"What's that got to do with anything?"

"Nothing. He's quick. I turned my back for a second..."

Kingsley laughed. His son had caught him like that as well. Hunter was right; he'd make a good running back one day. But only if Kingsley cleared up this mess with Stacia's murder. He didn't want Conner facing questions about his father in the pressroom someday.

Kingsley walked into the house carrying his son. He put him down when they were in the foyer.

"You heading out?" Kingsley asked.

"Yes. I'm going to stay at my place in Malibu for the next few weeks, but if you get any information I'll come back."

"Sounds good. I'll keep you posted. I've got Gabi moving in here and I think I should have something to go on soon."

"Good. The sooner we get to the bottom of the Stacia situation the better."

Hunter left and Kingsley watched his friend go until Conner tugged on his hand.

"Who's Stas?"

"An old friend of Daddy's. Good news, Con, we've got a new nanny coming to live with us."

"Like Peri?"

Nothing like Peri. For one thing, Kingsley had never gotten excited by the prospect of Peri living in his house. He tried to tell himself that he was only feeling that way because he could finally get to work on figuring out the past, but he knew it was lie.

He wanted more than that one night with Gabi. He wanted to know that what he remembered of their embrace had been real, and he wanted in his own mixed-up way to somehow make things up to her for their one-night stand.

Gabi paced her office for a few minutes after Kingsley left. She wasn't sure how it had happened but somehow she was back to being a nanny. A live-in nanny to a three-year-old she'd never met in the house of the only man she'd never been able to forget.

Ugh!

"Melissa, please draw up a contract for Mr. Buchanan," Gabi said as she walked into her assistant's office.

"I bet you're glad I let him in," Melissa said. "He is even hotter in person than he is on TV."

Yes, he was. There was no way a television could capture the force of his presence. But then, the meeting today hadn't taught her anything new.

"He did agree to fund the playground I've been lobbying for in town. And he wants me to start tonight."

"You? You don't work directly for clients anymore," Melissa said. "What happened in your office?"

This was what came of being too friendly with your staff. Melissa felt comfortable asking her anything she wanted.

"We used to know each other," Gabi admitted. "He offered to fund the playground if I took charge of his son and worked out of his home. This is going to take a lot of effort between you and me to make this happen. Because for the amount he's paying—he wants me there today."

Melissa put her elbows on her desk, leaning forward. "Oh, my God. Did he make you an indecent proposal? Are you going to be his mistress?"

"What? No! Where do you get these ideas?"

"I read a lot and watch a lot of soap operas," Melissa said with a wink. "So no to the bargaining with your body?"

She shook her head. "Definitely no. Just the playground and the stipulation that I live and work from his house. Which means that you are going to have to run things at this office. Think you can handle it?"

"Yes. You know I can."

Gabi did know. "It'll mean a raise for you, and I'm thinking that you will be my assistant manager. We will probably need to hire another assistant for you."

"Thank you, Gabi. I won't let you down," Melissa said.

"I know you won't."

"I'm going to call the county commissioners

and get an exact figure on the budget for the park. I want you to draw up our regular contract for a live-in nanny service and in place of the fees reference the addendum. I'll work on that."

"You said you have to be there tonight?"

Gabi kept her expression serene only after years of training, but inside she grimaced. Kingsley had doubled her workload for the day. "Yes. If I send you the dimensions of my new office, will you order me some furniture?"

"Yes. Are you sure about this?" Melissa asked. "We still have our fund-raising plan to get the play area built. I think we could do it without you having to jump through hoops."

Gabi was grateful to have Melissa not just as her assistant but also as her friend. "It would take years to raise that kind of money. This is easier. Besides, I could use some new material for my parenting column. All of my experience is several years old now."

"Always look on the bright side?"

"It's worked so far," Gabi said.

She reentered her office and felt a little better about the encounter with Kingsley. Then she got down to business. She left a message for Rupert Green, the county commissioner who was her contact on the playground. Then she texted Kingsley asking for the dimensions of her office, which he immediately texted back, also assuring her that he would furnish the space. She almost told him that she would do it herself, but she still had to pack her office and her personal belongings so she decided to let him handle it.

She managed to stay busy enough the entire day not to allow herself to think until she was driving out to Kingsley's house. Butterflies danced in her stomach and she had that stupid tingling in her body that she knew was from excitement. How could she be excited?

Kingsley.

She knew it would be useless to deny it. They had unfinished business between them. Ten years might have passed, but when he'd walked into her office today she'd felt like a college freshman again, starstruck by her first sight of the handsome quarterback.

But she'd learned that the golden boy wasn't untouchable. So why…

She shook her head. Was it possible that she was still crushing on him? That Kingsley Buchanan still had a hold over her despite the way he'd treated her? Not just ten years ago but today, arrogantly waltzing back into her life and making her feel again.

Awakening desires and passions she'd shoved to the darkest part of her soul in an attempt to never be that vulnerable again.

She had to remember that. How exposed he'd made her feel. She was stronger now. She had to be.

And there was little Conner to think about. She knew next to nothing about the boy, only that he was three and that Kingsley had used some of her methods with the toddler.

Great.

She was doing the very thing she'd warned nannies not to do for years. Going in blind.

She could justify it to Melissa by saying Kingsley was funding a playground that an economically disadvantaged community desperately needed. She could justify it to her mom by saying that getting back in the field would give her a better perspective for running her business.

But justifying it to herself just felt hollow. Like a lie. As she pulled to a stop in front of Kingsley's Spanish-style mansion, she admitted that she was here for one reason and one reason alone.

Kingsley had asked and she'd been unable to say no.

Kingsley had tried to get furniture that mirrored the stuff he'd seen in Gabi's office earlier but it turned out some of her pieces, such as the settee, were one of a kind. So he'd had to settle for some substitutions. All in all he was happy with the stuff he'd managed to get here on such short notice.

He was working under the desk connecting the computer and printer cords while his son lay on the floor nearby coloring.

Seven years younger than his older brother, Kingsley had been an "accident." His parents had gone back to work and sort of moved into a new phase of their lives when he was born.

He'd been left in the care of his nanny most of the time. And he wasn't complaining about that. But he'd never had much of a chance to just hang out with his father. Kingsley did his best to make sure that he and Conner did have plenty of time together.

"Daddy? How's this?" Conner brought a piece of copy paper that he'd been drawing on with his crayons over to him. The brightly colored scribbles were Conner's version of the view from their backyard. Kingsley had three of the images framed and hanging on his own office wall.

When he'd brought Conner into the office he was setting up for Gabi, his son had insisted on making her a picture—or rather, a "picter," as he said it.

"Looks good. I bet she'll love it."

Someone cleared her throat and Kingsley glanced up to see Gabi standing in the doorway. "The housekeeper let me in and told me where to find you."

He let his gaze skim over her from the floor up. She'd changed into a pair of white jeans that hugged her slim legs and a pretty turquoise blouse that was made out of some sort of flowing fabric. She had pulled her long caramel-colored hair back into a ponytail and wore a pair of flat sandals on her feet.

She squatted down, smiling at Conner. "Can I see your picture?"

"Yes."

He walked over to her with that toddler gait of his, sometimes speedy and a little unsteady. He handed her the photo and then went even closer, putting his hand on Gabi's knee as he pointed to the picture.

Kingsley swallowed as a rush of emotion he didn't want to define swamped him. Sometimes he got a punch of joy in the heart just watching Conner.

"This is the ocean and the sky. This is Daddy and Unca Hun."

"Unca Hun?"

"Hunter," Kingsley said.

"Of course. I'm Gabi," she said, turning her attention back to Conner. "I'm here to help your daddy take care of you."

"Like Peri."

Gabi glanced over at Kingsley and then turned back to the little boy. "Just like Peri. Did you help your daddy set up my office?"

He nodded and Gabi stood up, holding the paper loosely in her left hand. She held her right hand out to Conner.

Conner wasn't always good with strangers. There had been only a few people close to him since he'd been born. Pretty much Hunter and Peri. Then there were Kingsley's parents, who doted on Conner, but Jade's parents lived in Brazil and only saw Conner for a month each summer when they came to visit.

Kingsley took Gabi's hand and led her over to the desk. She looked at the surface, arching one eyebrow at him as she came to her mono-grammed stationery.

"How did you do all this?"

"I have my ways," he said. He was pleased with himself because he'd surprised her. It was important to ensure that Gabi was happy here, because he needed her to watch over Conner. He'd even sort of justified it to Hunter by say-ing that he needed her recollections of the night that Stacia had died. But deep inside he knew he'd gone through all of this effort on her office and in her bedroom because he'd wanted to show off a little.

To let Gabi see the life he'd made for himself. To hopefully dispel the image she might have been carrying of him for all these years—the image of him in handcuffs behind a glass wall.

"Time for dinner, Conner," Kingsley said. "Let's go find Mrs. Tillman while Gabi gets settled into her office. I'll be back shortly to give you the tour."

She nodded. "I have some boxes in my car that I need to bring in."

"I'll help once I get Conner settled."

"Bye," Conner said as he and Kingsley left the office. They headed down the hallway, Conner running ahead of Kingsley, as he was wont to do.

And when they entered the kitchen, he found Mrs. Tillman putting Conner's plate on the large farmhouse-style table in the corner of the breakfast nook. It had a built-in padded bench, which Conner scrambled up onto.

Kingsley usually made it a point to eat with

Conner when he was home, but tonight their schedule was slightly messed up. So Conner would be eating alone. Kingsley planned to dine with Gabi tonight to bring her up to speed on all the details of Conner's schedule. And because he wanted to get to know her again.

"Do you still need me to stay until bedtime?" Mrs. Tillman asked.

"Yes. I want to give Gabi time to settle in. Did you have a chance to introduce yourselves?"

"We did. I put her suitcase in her bedroom and after Conner's bath I will unpack it."

"That's okay, Mrs. Tillman," Gabi said from the doorway, a large brown box in her arms. "I can do it. Kingsley, do you have a hand truck I can use to bring my other office boxes in?"

"No, but I can help you carry them," he said.

"I don't want to disturb you," she said. "I can make a couple of trips."

She turned away and he realized it was too late—she'd already disturbed him and there was no coming back from that.

"Go on, Kingsley. I'll watch the scamp finish his dinner," Mrs. Tillman said.

"Is that okay, Con?"

"Yes."

Kingsley ruffled his son's hair and got to his feet, following after Gabi.

Three

"Everything Is Awesome" was blasting from the room next to hers. She had an idea that Conner was in there, but she doubted he was alone. She'd done a good job of avoiding being alone with Kingsley. But she had to admit it had been harder than she'd expected.

He'd followed her to her car and if Hunter hadn't called just then perhaps she would have found herself on the patio under the moonlit sky having dinner with this complicated man from her past. But Hunter had saved her from that. She'd escaped into the house and then into a shower and avoided Kingsley for the rest of the night.

But at 6:00 a.m. everything didn't feel awesome. As the nanny, she knew she needed to check on Conner. So she jumped out of bed and walked into his room. He was sitting quietly in his bed with a book open on his lap.

She turned the volume down on his radio before walking over to his toddler bed.

"Morning, kiddo. What are you doing?"

"Reading. Peri likes it if we start the morning quiet," he said softly.

"I'm not Peri," Gabi said, sitting on the edge of his bed and glancing over at the book. It was a picture book—*One Fish Two Fish Red Fish Blue Fish* by Dr. Seuss. She smiled as she noticed that he was rubbing his finger over the pictures and not really reading. But then he was only three, a little young for true reading.

"Do you like this one?" she asked.

"Yes. Daddy took me fishing in summer."

"Did you catch a red or blue fish?"

He laughed at her. "Nope. They were brown."

She ruffled his hair. "They usually are."

His room was neat and she noticed that someone had laid his clothes out for the day on a chair facing the window. She suspected that Conner had opened the curtains because they were only parted nearest the floor.

"What do you want to do today?"

He looked up at her, and it was odd seeing the innocence in a pair of eyes that reminded her very strongly of Kingsley. King had never been that innocent. Never.

"Can we go to the beach? Daddy and I walk in the morning after breffest."

She smiled and nodded. "Where do we eat breakfast?"

"In the kitchen with Mrs. Tillman. I have to finish my book first," he said.

"Want to read it to me?" she asked.

He nodded. "Uncle Hun taught me a rap."

Hunter was seemingly full of surprises. She chastised herself for thinking that. To be honest, she'd never really known Hunter, just his reputation, which prior to Stacia's death had been one of a charming Romeo, playful, sexy and fun.

It was only afterward that she'd started to have doubts about him.

"I'd love to hear it."

Conner grinned up at her and then pushed the covers down and stood up on his bed. "Gimme a beat."

She had no idea how to beatbox. She wasn't too sure she'd have the nerve to ever try doing this if her audience was anyone other than a toddler, but he was waiting for her and she didn't want to let him down.

She made some beat noises and heard laughter from the door behind her.

"Finally we find the one thing that Gabi can't do," Kingsley said from the doorway. His hair was damp, presumably from his shower, and he had on a pair of faded jeans and a faded Buffalo Bills T-shirt. His feet were bare.

"Daddy, can you gimme a beat?"

Kingsley nodded. Gabi pretended not to notice how his shirt clung to his thickly muscled arms or the way he walked over to the bed.

Conner started jumping and rapping Dr. Seuss's timeless story. She had to admit she fell a little in love with Conner, and that cold lump in the pit of her stomach that had to do with old bitterness and resentment started to loosen.

For the first time since she left the jailhouse ten years ago she felt a spark of something like real emotion. She'd never been able to let a man get close to her after what Kingsley had done. Caution should be her watchword, but instead she wanted to throw it to the wind and find a little of the innocence she'd seen in Conner's eyes in her own life and in Kingsley's.

Every morning since his son was born Kingsley had woken with the desire to put the past to rest. This morning was no exception. As he'd lain in his bed watching the small bit of sun shining in through the crack in his blinds and realizing he was back in California, he'd felt the familiar anger and determination rise inside him.

He needed answers and if he were being totally honest, revenge against whomever had killed Stacia and set Hunter and him up. But rapping with his son and Gabi first thing in the morning brought peace to some long-forgotten part of his soul. A part he thought had died a long time ago.

As Conner finished rapping about the fish and did his "gangsta" pose, Gabi applauded. The little boy looked as if he'd swallowed the sun. He wasn't immune to Gabi, either.

Kingsley's entire life had been set on course by the actions of someone else. His silver-spoon existence had been taken away but he'd done his best to claw his way back, and having Conner made it all the more important that he succeed. But when he stood here near Gabi he had a glimpse of a life that might have been. Something he could have had if life hadn't been so cruel.

Damn. He was feeling sorry for himself and he couldn't tolerate that.

"I can get Conner ready if you want to get dressed and then we can go have breakfast."

"Yippee!" Conner said, dancing around.

"Okay, but isn't this my job?" she asked.

Kingsley nodded. "We need to get your schedule figured out. I have a meeting this afternoon with a potential client and I have to fly out for a few days after that. But we can discuss that over breakfast. I did promise you'd have time to do your work, as well."

Gabi crossed her arms under her breasts. He was trying to ignore how sexy she looked in a sleeveless navy blue T-shirt and a pair of long, flowing pajama pants. But he wasn't doing a great job. Frankly, he knew that it was a cliché to hit on his son's nanny, but in this case he'd known Gabi way before she'd been Conner's nanny.

Still, he knew that hitting on her wasn't going to go over well. And he was smoother than that. Really, he was. No matter how kissable she looked. In fact, she looked like the woman he remembered from college. She wasn't wearing any makeup and the tough, businesslike facade she had worn yesterday was gone, leaving in its place a woman he wanted to cuddle up to.

"Why are you staring at me?" she asked as Conner went over to his closet to find his beach shoes.

"Because I want to kiss you."

"You aren't going to act on that, because the

contract I sent over prohibits fraternization between the nanny and anyone in the house."

"That's why I struck that clause out. Whatever happens between us started a long time ago."

Conner came back out of his closet.

"We can discuss this later. You aren't going to get your way every time we negotiate."

"We'll see," he said.

Gabi walked away and Kingsley watched as she firmly closed the door between her room and Conner's.

"I like her," Conner said.

"Me, too," Kingsley admitted to his son. He helped Conner change and then supervised him brushing his teeth and washing his face.

He was always struck by how quickly Conner was growing. It wasn't that long ago that Kingsley would have had to do both chores for him. But now he was independent enough to do them himself.

"Daddy?"

"Yes?"

"Are you ready for breffest?"

"Yeah, Con, I am. Let's go." Kingsley reached

out to his son and felt that tiny hand grip his so securely. Whatever went down in the next few months it was paramount to Kingsley that Conner—and by extension, Gabi—was protected. Obviously, some stray sparks had burned her when Stacia died. Finding Stacia's real killer, clearing his name once and for all and making sure that justice was served…that was a tall order. But one that King and Hunter felt sure they were up to.

Hunter had heard that their old football coach had retired and was living in Carmel not too far from Kingsley's new home. Hunter planned to visit the old man and see what he remembered. The party where Stacia was killed had been held at his home on campus.

"What time are you leaving today?" Gabi asked as he entered the kitchen. He noticed that she had a bowl of cereal and fresh fruit prepared for Conner.

Conner scampered up onto the bench seat and started eating.

"Not until this afternoon."

"I need to run back to my office and sign some

papers and I'd like to bring my assistant out here so she knows how to get here. It was a little complicated and Melissa isn't the best with her GPS."

Kingsley was irritated. He wanted Gabi here. That was what he'd paid for, but he was aware of how well saying something like that would go over. He needed her and he was willing to let her go for now. "Okay, but I want lunch, just you and me. Mrs. Tillman will watch Conner. We need to get a few details settled before I leave."

"What details?"

"We can discuss it at lunch," he said. He wanted to be alone with Gabi. He didn't question it. He'd been operating by his gut for a long time and it hadn't let him down—except for that one night with Stacia.

He was determined to put the past to rest and to make things up to Gabi. But he knew deep inside that it was her icy exterior that made him want to do it. He wanted to crack through it and find the young woman who'd been so in love with him that she'd come to visit him in jail.

* * *

Gabi had done her best to avoid Kingsley and she felt like a coward. But standing on the threshold of the terrace in the sun with the gorgeous view of the Pacific in the background, she was almost glad she was here. She'd come out here not just to be a nanny to Conner, but also to put the past to rest for once. Her mother was always keen to point out that she kept all men at arm's length.

She dated.

She was a woman and had needs and got tired of her own company, so of course she'd been out on dates and even hooked up occasionally. But she had yet to be with a man for more than one night, and she had studied enough psychology to recognize that pattern for what it was. Kingsley had left a part of her scarred when he'd rejected her.

So she was here in part to heal. To somehow bring closure to that one-night stand they'd had and hopefully make it possible for her to have a real relationship and give her mom those grandkids she was desperate for.

"I wasn't sure you'd come."

"Why not? I like to eat just as much as the next person."

"This isn't just about the meal. You've been avoiding being alone with me since you moved into my house," he said.

He wore a pair of perfectly tailored dress pants and a button-down shirt that had been cut to his size. Kingsley wore his wealth well. And she had to admit that she admired him for it. She was sick of seeing men in baggy jeans on the streets. Kingsley took pride in his appearance and she liked it.

She'd worn a sleeveless sheath dress in turquoise that her mother had told her brought out her eyes. Her mom spent a lot of her time making sure Gabi was presentable to the world.

Kingsley led the way to the table and held a chair out for her. She sort of regretted missing dinner last night. She'd feigned sleepiness and gone to bed early. But she'd needed time to shore up her barriers. To focus on what was important—the kids who'd get the playground that his fee was paying for. Conner, who needed a nanny focused on the job of caring for him and not his superhot dad. And rebuilding her shattered feminine self-worth. That was why she'd stayed away, but today, with the sun shining and Kingsley sitting next to her looking as though he'd stepped out of one of her dreams, it was hard to remember any of that.

"Why are you back in California?" she asked. Get to know him. Wasn't that the first thing every *Cosmo* quiz told a woman to do? It was also what she had decided she needed to help herself get over him.

"I wanted Conner to grow up with the sea and the sun. Plus, my parents haven't forgiven me for…"

"Stacia?" she asked. She wasn't going to pretend he didn't have that in his past. It was the incident that defined them as a couple. Three weeks of dating culminating in a one-night stand. And she suspected she needed some closure on that, as well. "What did happen that night?"

"I don't… Are you sure you want to talk about it?" he asked.

"Yes. I thought… Well, that doesn't matter. I remember that you took me home and stayed until my roommate came back and then you left. What happened next?"

He rubbed the back of his neck and took a long sip of his sparkling water before he put his elbows on the table and leaned forward. "I took a long walk around the campus. I didn't want to go back to the frat house or the party. I needed to think."

"What about?"

"You, Gabi. You were a freshman and I was a senior. My life was on track at that point. You know the draft was my next goal, but then you came along and things sort of changed."

"How?"

"You were different and it made me think about something other than football for a while," he said.

She wanted to believe him. There was no reason for him to lie to her at this moment, but if that was the truth, why had he been so cruel to her at the jailhouse?

"Yeah, right. Listen, we both know I was just

some dewy-eyed coed that you saw as an easy score," she said. "You don't have to put a different spin on it. I was more than willing to go with you that night."

"Believe what you will, but that night was special for me. You were different," he said.

"Then why were you so mean when I came to visit you?" she asked. There had been no reason for that.

"I was protecting you. I had no clear memories of the night before. I only knew that I'd been found with Stacia and Hunter and that she had been killed. The cops were trying to implicate me in some sort of twisted sex game, and I wanted you as far from that as I could get you," he said.

She swallowed hard. "Really?"

"Would I lie about that? I certainly didn't leave you and go back to the party to kill Stacia."

"What did happen? Do you know?"

"I don't," he said. "We've never found out anything other than they had no evidence to prosecute Hunter and me. Both of us can't recall the night that clearly. What about you? Do you remember anything from that night?" he asked.

"Just being into you and around you," she said. She tipped her head to the side to study him. Stacia's death was still like a fresh wound to Kingsley. Gabi could tell by the way he was talking about it. Hear it in the anger in his voice.

"If you can remember anything from that night that seemed odd," he said, "I'd like to know about it."

"Why?"

"Hunter and I have been piecing together stories and memories of that night. Hunter and Stacia were serious about each other. He blames himself for her death."

"Did he kill her?"

"No. He didn't," Kingsley said. "Enough about that. Tell me about your business. How did you go from college to being a nanny?"

She put her hand on his and squeezed it. That knot of anger that had been deep inside her since the moment she'd woken to hear that her lover had been arrested for killing another woman eased. It had been a long time in coming, but she finally felt as if she was seeing Kingsley as the man he could be.

She didn't trust herself. Didn't know if she ever would be able to again, but there was a little bit of hope inside her now.

Four

Talking about the night Stacia died always made Kingsley feel anger and resentment. He'd had it all until then. He'd felt untouchable—in part thanks to his family's money. School had come easily to him and he'd been on the dean's list every semester. He hadn't won the Heisman Trophy, but he had been mentioned as a first-round draft pick. His life had been, well, charmed, and he'd taken it for granted.

He'd slept with Gabi, knowing that she came from a good family. He had imagined she'd be the perfect accoutrement for the idyllic life he pictured for himself. One where he outshone his older brother, where after he'd won the Super Bowl he'd retire and have the perfect family. He figured he'd play hard and when Gabi graduated he'd think about settling down with her.

But after the arrest those plans had disappeared. He'd been shocked that he hadn't been able to talk the cops out of arresting both him and Hunter. It had been inconceivable that anyone would think Hunter would have killed Stacia. Despite his name, Hunter didn't really have a killer instinct. Which is how they'd ended up being labeled the Frat House Killers.

Sitting in the sun with Gabi just reinforced his need for revenge. To find out who had killed Stacia and make them pay for the plans they'd interrupted, for the life they'd taken. And the years they'd lived with the stigma of being murderers.

Gabi pushed her sunglasses up to the top of her head and leaned forward.

"You look scary. Is that your don't-sack-me face?"

He forced a smile because he could tell that was what she wanted, but this lunch simply reinforced all he'd lost. If he hadn't been accused of murder, maybe he would have married better. Maybe Conner's mother would still be alive if he hadn't been so…uninterested in anything except making enough money so he could go after his revenge.

"Yeah. You'd be amazed at what it takes to stop a three-hundred-pound linebacker."

"I shudder to think of facing someone like that. I'm sorry I brought up Stacia. I can tell that it still bothers you," she said.

"Her killer was never brought to justice. Someone thought that Hunter and I would take the fall for them. They were wrong," he said.

"Maybe the cops will find that person," Gabi said.

Doubtful. Especially since most of them believed he and Hunter had gotten off because of their family money. But he didn't want to get into that with Gabi. He needed to know if she remembered anything else about that night. Hunter thought someone might have drugged them before Stacia was killed. Gabi was still on campus after the party, so she might have heard something along those lines. But for right now he wanted to enjoy this lunch.

He'd had some hot dreams about Gabi last night. Maybe it was the fact that they'd only had that one night together or maybe it was because she was under his roof again, but he wanted her. He wanted to see if the kiss, the sex he remembered with her had been real. Or just another illusion that would be shattered by reality.

"You're staring again."

"I'm wondering what it would be like to kiss you," he said.

She flushed under her tan and licked her lips. Her mouth had fascinated him from the first moment he'd met her. Her lips were full and lush. She'd never worn lipstick in college and now she wore something that made her lips shimmer but didn't add color to them.

"Well, stop wondering. I'm in your house to be a nanny, not to assuage your curiosity."

He threw his head back and laughed. "Assuage?"

"Yes, got a problem with it?"

"Not at all. It's just that I figured since you worked with kids—"

"I'd talk like a toddler?" she asked.

He shook his head. She rattled him and made his legendary charm disappear. It was unnerving and at the same time exciting. She was still different from every other woman he'd ever known.

"My curiosity still needs to be assuaged."

She shook her head and lifted the cloche off the plate in front of her. "I have to get to my meeting, so let's eat."

"Don't like talking about kissing me?" he asked.

He took his lid off as well and saw that Mrs. Tillman had prepared fish tacos. His favorite. Gabi took a bite and chewed carefully.

Hell, he needed to kiss her and take her to his bed. Get over this odd infatuation he had with her. What else could he call watching her chew and thinking it was cute?

He took a bite of his taco, glad as hell that Hunter had gone to Malibu for a few weeks. He didn't want his friend to see him mooning over Gabi.

Was that what he was doing?

"So, while you are gone, is it okay to ask your housekeeper to watch Conner if I need to have a conference call?" she asked. "I will do my writing and paperwork either while Conner is having his nap or at night while he's sleeping. But I'm in the middle of placing two nannies with some rather high-profile clients and I don't want to lose their business."

"Yes, that will be fine. She's not interested in being a full-time nanny but will help out as needed."

"Great. Now, when will you be back?"

"In a week. Do you feel like you can handle Conner?"

"Certainly. He seems pretty well adjusted. You've done a good job with raising him," she said.

"I had some excellent advice," he said. "I bought your book."

She shook her head. "Lots of people have bought my book and still have kids that are out of control. You seem to actually listen to him, which is key."

"Well, I like my son," Kingsley said.

"That's a good thing."

"I like you, too," he said.

"Don't. We have a business relationship."

"I know that. But what's to preclude us from having more?"

"Common sense," she said.

Maybe it was being back in Cali or just being around Gabi, but he felt young again. Free in a way he hadn't been since their one night together. She made him want to be the man who had dreams. Not the man who was focused on vengeance.

But the dreamer was gone. And he was a taker now.

He wanted Gabi.

She kept him at arm's length, which was one thing he wasn't going to allow. She was part of the reason he was here. Not just revenge.

Okay, that wasn't entirely true. But now that she was under his roof, his focus was changing. He still craved revenge on whoever had set Hunter and him up, but he also desperately wanted Gabi.

It was her fault.

She sat across from him in the midday California sun, watching him as though she wanted more, too.

Maybe she'd been waiting, too. Waiting for him to come back into her life.

Yeah, right.

Hell.

What if she was involved with someone? Why wouldn't she be?

"Do you have a boyfriend?" he asked. "Is that why you are busy espousing common sense?"

She shook her head. "So the only reason a woman wouldn't want to throw away her professionalism with you is because she's involved with someone else?"

"This feels like a trap," he said. "I just wanted to know if there was a man in your life."

"There are a lot of them," she said.

That didn't fit with the woman he thought he knew. But then he had to admit that reading her column and her book didn't give him any special insight into her personal life.

"Fair enough."

She laughed in a very kind way. It was something he hadn't heard in a long time. Women didn't usually laugh around him.

"What?"

"You are so transparent."

"Am I?"

"Yes."

"What do you see?" he asked her. He had the feeling she was toying with him and that feeling of being free took him again. It had been a long time since anyone had teased him.

"I see a man who wants to kiss me."

"I told you that," he said.

"But you aren't the kind of man who'd poach so you want to know if I'm taken."

"What's wrong with that?"

"Nothing. It makes me like you a little bit more."

That sounded like a good thing, but with Gabi he wasn't sure. "Thanks."

"Don't sound scared. It is a good thing. You

came into my office trying to get your own way instead of asking the way most people would. So why are you being so polite about this?" she asked.

Damn.

Of course she'd see what few others did. He rubbed the back of his neck and the feeling of freedom slipped away. The chains of the past were once again wrapped around his neck and ankles. Tying him to that one night, that one event. He didn't want to tell her that it was the fact that Stacia had been raped that night that had also stayed with him. The DNA evidence had been inconclusive and he had no memory of sleeping with anyone other than Gabi, but he wanted to give no woman the chance to say he'd taken her against her will.

"Let's just say consent is a biggie in my book," he said.

"It is in mine, too. But one kiss, Kingsley—I wouldn't begrudge that."

"If I took it you might later," he said.

She put her hand on his. "Do you know why I'm afraid to let go of common sense?"

He had a few thoughts on the matter—she might not want to kiss him, which, given the sexual attraction he felt around her, he hoped wasn't the case. She might have a boyfriend, but he was beginning to think that wasn't the case, either. But the real reason? Only Gabi knew that. She protected her secrets behind her pretty brown eyes like an armed security guard.

"Not really."

"You make me forget all of the caution I carefully built into myself over the last ten years. You make me want to be the freshman girl who took a senior football player back to her dorm room. And that's not smart. And this is the tricky part—I usually think of myself as a smart woman, so kissing you...well, that would be dumb."

He realized she was talking and rationalizing to keep herself safe. Hell, he didn't blame her, but every male instinct he had was saying she was his. He'd claimed her that night all those years ago and he wanted her back again.

But he had a son.

He had a mission in California.

He owed Hunter and himself a chance to clear their names.

Something he knew he couldn't do if he took Gabi to his bed again. She cluttered his mind. She made him want things he had lived a long time without.

But one kiss?

Surely, one kiss wouldn't do that much damage.

One kiss.

"One kiss," he said.

"What?"

"One kiss. That's all I'm asking for. What could it hurt? We are both wondering if our memories are right and if that fire between us was really as scorching hot as we remember."

"Are we?" she asked, but she took her sunglasses off her head, set them on the table next to her plate and put her hands on the armrests of her chair as if she were about to stand.

"Yes. You know it and I do, too. Common sense isn't going to withstand curiosity," he said.

"You're right," she admitted, standing up and walking over to him.

He scooted his chair back and before he could stand, she sat on his lap, wrapping her arms around him and tangling her hands in the hair at the back of his neck. Last time she'd been in his arms she'd been a girl, scared and unsure. This time she was a woman and knew what she wanted.

"One kiss, Kingsley. Better make it count."

He intended to.

Gabi knew she'd dared him to kiss her. Okay, so maybe she thought that way she'd be able to say he'd forced her into it later, though she knew that wasn't true.

There weren't many things she truly wanted for herself but Kingsley was one of them. There was no denying that despite the coldhearted way he'd dumped her at the police station she still wanted him. Still wanted this embrace.

She wanted to tell herself that he'd been so cruel that night because he'd been trying to protect her, but deep inside she had to admit that even if he hadn't, he was still hot. Still the one man she looked at and felt the kind of sexual longing that made her forget common sense and reason. He made her want to act like…well, like this.

Sitting on his lap in the midafternoon California sun for the entire world to see. Except there wasn't anyone else around. It was just the two of them.

She'd never really had Kingsley to herself during their brief courtship. He'd been big man on campus and everywhere they'd gone people knew him, had high-fived him and wanted to talk to him.

This was different.

He was different.

Hell, so was she. She'd been different for a long time now. But suddenly his mouth moved over hers and she forgot all of that.

Forgot to think and to worry.

Forgot to justify this because his mouth felt so good, so right as he parted his lips and his tongue slipped over her teeth.

She tightened her fingers on his shoulders. God, the man was still solid muscle.

But then his bespoke suits had already sort of

hinted at that and she'd seen him in that tight T-shirt last night. He was fit. He always had been and she wanted to tear off his shirt and see the body beneath his clothes.

She shut her eyes as he put his hands on either side of her face and deepened the kiss. Everything feminine inside her clenched and then released. It felt as if her blood flow was heavier in her veins and her heart was racing. She heard the sound of her heart beating in her ears like the distant call of warning drums.

She knew she should tear her mouth from his, get up and walk away, but instead she brought her hands closer to his neck, brushed her fingers over his short beard and then ran her fingers over his jaw.

She wanted this kiss to last forever.

She needed to keep tasting him to somehow figure out if this was just another sort of dream that she was having. Like the foggy memories of their night together. This felt too good. Too intense. It couldn't be real. No man kissed like this.

No man had this kind of power over her.

She pulled back, opened her eyes and looked up at Kingsley. His eyes were half-closed, but she saw the fabulous blue of his irises.

He was her Achilles' heel. He was the one person who could make her behave in a way that she knew better. For some reason he'd always found his way around her will and with no great effort.

Why?

What kind of hold did he have over her?

And why the hell was it still there? She thought ten years would have dulled his magnetism, but that wasn't the case. If anything he was more captivating now. His kiss was more thorough than it had been in college.

She leaned closer to him. Put her arms around his shoulders and rested her cheek on it. She didn't want to look at him. Didn't want to kiss him again. And there was a very real worry that she would do just that.

"Kingsley."

"Gabriella," he said. Just her name in that low tone fanned the fires already burning deep inside her. She shook her head, pushed herself upright and started to get off his lap, but he put his hands on her waist.

She knew she could have escaped and dammit, she didn't want to. She liked the feel of him holding her. Keeping her close.

"That cannot happen again," she said at last.

"Not good enough?" he asked, arching one eyebrow arrogantly at her.

He knew it was plenty good enough. The bastard.

"I think we both know it couldn't get much better."

"Unless we were both naked," he said.

She bit her lower lip, tasted him on her and closed her eyes. How was she going to live in his house and not give in to this temptation again?

She'd never in all of her years of nannying been tempted by a father. Never thought about maybe hooking up with one. But Kingsley wasn't just a client to her. She knew Kingsley. Remembered what he looked like naked, and dammit if she wasn't ready to see him that way again. She knew she had a responsibility to Conner. And she'd be the best nanny that little boy ever had.

And there was only one way to do that. She pushed herself to her feet and walked back around to her side of the table. No more flirting.

No more giving in to her stupid curiosity.

No more kissing Kingsley.

He was still just watching her as she plucked her sunglasses off the table and put them on.

"Well, that was interesting."

Interesting? That was one way to describe it. Gabi thought it was dangerous, intoxicating, and she knew she was going to have to be on her guard every moment to prevent a repeat performance.

"I guess."

"You guess?"

She shrugged. She was trying to walk a fine line here. Professionalism had failed as a barrier to keep him at arm's length and it didn't seem as though dares were working well, either. It was only the stiff formal behavior her mother had drummed into her that kept her sitting there smiling as if nothing was wrong when inside she was on fire and felt that she'd made a very dangerous misstep.

Five

His phone rang. He hit the ignore button when he saw it was Hunter. Gabi gave him a quizzical look.

"It's Hunter. I'll call him later."

"You two are pretty close, aren't you?" she asked. She was sipping delicately at her water.

There was nothing sexy about drinking water, but somehow there was when she did it. He couldn't tear his eyes from her mouth as she put the glass back on the table and licked her lips.

She'd hidden her big brown eyes from him with her sunglasses and he wondered what she was thinking. This Gabi was very good at hiding what she felt. She wasn't at all like the hot-tempered girl he remembered. The one who'd let him have it if he as much as looked at another girl. She had told him she deserved a man who wasn't playing the field and if he didn't agree he could hit the road.

"So you never said if you were dating anyone," he said.

"Would I have kissed you if I were?"

He shrugged. He didn't think so, but why make assumptions? He wanted to hear from her own lips that she was single—and available to him.

"I don't know. It's been ten years."

"Fair enough. I have changed a bit, but not about that. I believe if you commit yourself to a relationship then you honor it."

"Me, too."

She arched one eyebrow at him. "Don't say that if you don't mean it. It was just a kiss—"

"It was more than a kiss, Gabi. It was a reaffirmation that there is still something white-hot between us."

She bit her lower lip. "Damn."

"What?"

"I was hoping that you didn't feel it, too."

"I'd have to be dead not to have felt it," he said. "Why did you want that?"

"Because I'm Conner's nanny. I'm here as a professional in your home, not to date you," she said. "I've never been tempted to mix business and pleasure and I'm not sure it's a wise idea now."

"I don't think it's a dumb idea," he said, trying for his most charming grin.

She shook her head. "That's because you're a man."

"Hey, that's not fair."

"But it's true."

He had to grin at her. She made him feel alive again. Something that he usually only experienced with Conner and his very small inner circle of employees and friends—Peri, Mrs. Tillman and Hunter.

Was this real, or was he feeling something from the past for Gabi?

She'd believed in his innocence back then and that had meant a lot to him.

"I think we can both handle this. I trust you to

be a good nanny to Conner whatever happens between us."

"I'm not sure, Kingsley. How would you feel about maybe giving this a break until I'm not living in your home? I have to set a good example for the women who work for me. I have a strict no-fraternization policy," she said.

He had another glimpse of the woman Gabi was now. He had sort of seen those differences in the articles she'd written and in her office. She was a success in a business she'd built from the ground up. She came from a very wealthy family who were related to the Spanish royals, so she'd never needed to work. Yet she did.

She worked hard.

He didn't want to do anything that would harm her reputation or call her ethics into question.

But he wanted her.

He had been searching his entire adult life for a woman who could make him feel this way, and no other one had. He knew that he had another agenda and that his focus should be on clearing his and Hunter's names. Making whoever was responsible for Stacia's death pay. But sitting here in the Cali sun with Gabi made all that seem distant.

Suddenly getting revenge on the real killer wasn't as important as making sure he could kiss Gabi again and hold her in his arms. Make love to her until they both forget everything except the way it felt to be wrapped around each other.

His phone beeped and he saw it was a text message from Hunter.

WTF. Are you really romancing the nanny? I thought we decided that we'd fix the past.

Damn.

He glanced at Gabi.

"I have to respond to this."

"It's okay. I think we need a break. I'm going to go inside and find Conner. He is supposed to have a nap in twenty minutes, so I should be there."

"How did you know?"

"I emailed Peri last night. She sent his schedule," Gabi said. "Thanks for lunch and for that kiss."

She walked away and he watched her. She wasn't doing anything to turn him on, just walking away. But he couldn't tear his eyes from her body. Could barely make himself stay in his chair.

And that was as big a wake-up call as Hunter's text. Kingsley had come here for answers and for revenge. He needed to remember that.

Soon Conner would start school, and sooner or later it would come out that his father was an accused murderer. And he wanted better than that for his son. He didn't want him to have to deal with that.

And no matter how good Gabi felt in his arms, he needed peace of mind. He needed to clear his name and put the past to rest before he moved on. He knew that.

Hell, he'd never had any problem doing that until her. What was it about Gabi that shook him that way?

He picked up his phone.

Your timing could be better. How did you know I was with Gabi?

I know you. Is this still a priority for you?

Yes. I'm flying to the East Coast to meet with Daria Miller. She was one of Stacia's sorority sisters. I read a blog post she wrote about the college drug culture. I want to talk to her about her experience.

Great. I'm going to follow up on Coach. He's in the hospital.

Sounds good. Talk to you soon.

He put his phone on the table and looked at the empty spot where Gabi had been sitting. He wanted her. He was trying to—hell, he wasn't going to tell himself that lie. He wasn't doing anything but waiting for her. And he had to put that aside. Revenge and new relationships really didn't mix.

Gabi made sure Conner was sleeping before she retreated to her office. She had a video monitor so she could keep an eye on him, and according to Peri, Conner was good for a forty-five-minute nap. That meant she had just enough time to finish the draft of a speech she was giving next weekend to the Young Women's Business Association.

So why was she on the internet doing a Google search on Kingsley, Hunter and Stacia? But she knew why. He'd made her curious when he'd brought up college. She'd taken a break from college for a year shortly after Kingsley had been arrested and gone to Spain to visit her cousin Gui.

It had been nice to spend time with Gui and Kara. The escape from her real-life problems had been welcome, and when she'd returned home after spending time with her little niece, her mom had volunteered her to nanny for Mal and his family. She'd been too busy to follow the story except when Hunter and Kingsley had been released from jail. And then Kingsley had been drafted and went to New York to play pro football.

And now he was back. Why?

He'd said he was back because he wanted to raise Conner in the California sun, but Kingsley had grown up in Connecticut. True, given the past few winters it made sense that he'd want to be out here where they weren't snowed in for weeks. Her gut was saying there was more to it than that.

She read all the past articles on the original incident. She knew from her own memories of the night that the party had been wild. She'd been focused on Kingsley, having made up her mind that they'd finally have sex. So she really hadn't seen much of Hunter or Stacia.

Kingsley and she had left early. And that had been what she'd wanted.

"Got a minute?"

She minimized her search window and smiled over at Kingsley where he stood in the doorway.

"Sure. What's up?"

"I wanted to remind you that I'm going to be out of town for a week. I'll leave after Conner wakes up from his nap. I don't want to go without saying goodbye."

That was sweet. He was a good father. Was he a good man? That was the question that kept spinning through her mind. Every time she thought she had him figured out he did something else.

Like that lunch. He'd been funny, sort of sweet and oh, so charming. Everything any woman would want from a date...

She was afraid she was waiting for the other shoe to fall. Experience had taught her that things never went smoothly with Kingsley.

"Okay. I will have to work around my schedule. I might need to take Conner to my office in Carmel a few days. I have a play area there. And it would only be for a few hours. But I wasn't planning to be away this long," she said.

"That's fine. I did spring this on you. We can work out a better schedule when I get back," he said. He handed her a business card with his contact numbers.

She took it, turned it over in her hand. Something was different.

Something had changed in him since she'd left the patio.

"Is everything okay?"

"Yes, why wouldn't it be?"

"Because you were all, *let's have an affair*, and

now you're handing me your business card and dashing out the door," she said. "What's up?"

"I'm respecting your wishes. You said you couldn't do this while nannying my son."

She narrowed her eyes, watching him carefully and trying to gauge if he was lying to her. She had asked for the space. Just because she'd sort of counted on him not giving it to her was no reason to get upset now. Except, dammit, he'd kissed her. Gotten her turned on and made her believe that he was going to be pursuing her. Now he was turning it off.

Something had changed.

What?

Hunter. Hunter had called him earlier. Maybe there was bad news from his friend.

"Is everything okay with Hunter?"

"Yes. Why do you ask?"

She put his card down and walked around the desk so she could lean against the front of it. She noticed whenever she moved that he watched her hips and her legs. He'd always been a leg man. Though she was dressed conservatively, Kingsley's eyes on her made her feel as if she was wearing a micro-miniskirt and rocking it.

"You've changed," she said, crossing her legs at the ankles. The slim-fitting skirt pulled tight around her thighs. She noticed his gaze skim down to it before he looked away from her.

"What do you want?" he asked. "Did you say no so I'd push you? You know I'm not that kind of man."

She nodded. "I do know that. I wasn't saying no so much as…trying to see if you were serious or just toying with me. This feels like you don't know, either."

Talking about it made it all clearer. She did want him to keep coming after her. She'd gone to see him and bared her soul as a young girl and he'd rejected her. She hadn't thought that she was still carrying that scar around, but it turned out it hadn't faded as much as she'd hoped.

Instead she was afraid to be pushed aside again. She hoped that was it. Hoped it wasn't that some part of her wanted to reject him.

"We have a lot of history, Gabi, not all of it good. I am here in Cali for work but also to put the ghosts of the past to rest. I guess while we were having lunch I felt like the man I might have been. Thank you for that."

Her heart melted a little. While it was easy to focus on her feelings, it was harder to see things from Kingsley's point of view. He'd lost a lot the night he'd been arrested.

"You're welcome. I want us to at least be friends again," she said.

"Friends?"

She nodded.

"It's a start," he said. "But don't kid yourself. I'm never going to be satisfied being just your friend."

He closed the gap between them and kissed her with all the passion she remembered from that night so long ago. All the restraint he'd showed on the patio was gone. The kiss was carnal and then he pulled back, rubbed his thumb over her lips and walked away. She was shattered.

Kingsley stood in Conner's doorway and watched his son sleep. His dad had once said there was no greater joy and agony than having a child. Kingsley had simply heard the regret in his old man's voice and felt the guilt of his own failings. But recently he was starting to understand where the old man was coming from.

He wanted so much for his son. So much more than he could give him. He wanted to protect him and to give him everything he never had. But he'd had a lot of advantages. He wasn't sure how he was going to keep Conner from ending up in the wrong place at the wrong time as he had.

That fear was always in the back of his mind. He hadn't been a saint in college, but he'd certainly never pushed a girl to be with him—or drugged her. Both things were key in Stacia's death. The cold case had left open the option that maybe after a night of crazy drinking and drugging Stacia had taken her own life. But Hunter didn't believe it.

And neither did Kingsley.

He went into Conner's room, trying to shake off memories of the past. This little guy was the future. The driving force behind him being here.

That and revenge. He wanted the person who'd tainted his future to pay for what he'd done.

He wasn't going to sugarcoat it. He wanted to ruin whoever had framed Hunter and him, and he knew that nothing was going to sway him from his mission. Not Gabi and her sexy legs. Not even Conner.

He needed revenge. His moral compass didn't always skew the same as most people's, but in this he was damned sure of his path.

Hunter was right. He was distracted with Gabi. But he also knew he wasn't going to send her away. To ask her to send another nanny so he wouldn't be…what? Conflicted.

Damn.

"Daddy?"

"Right here, buddy. How was your nap?" he asked, sitting down on Conner's toddler bed that was shaped like a race car. One of his friends was the F1 driver Marco Moretti, and Marco had sent the bed to Conner as a gift for his last birthday.

Kingsley rubbed the back of his neck. He had a good life. A life he'd carved for himself out of the ashes of that arrest. The only loose end was the person who'd done it and why.

He wanted to know why. Hunter needed it, too. He felt as if he was responsible for Stacia. And while Kingsley had Conner and a group of good friends, Hunter hadn't allowed himself to care for anyone since Stacia's death.

It had haunted his friend.

"Good. I like Gammi."

"Gabi, buddy, her name is Gabi."

"That's what I said. Gammi."

He rubbed Conner's head. He'd read an article that said to gently correct speech mistakes but not make a big deal of them. Then the child would just struggle to speak. So he let it go. He had nicknames for many people in his life.

"I've got to go to a meeting on the East Coast. Gabi and Mrs. Tillman are going to watch you. Gabi might need to go to her office to work and you'll get to go with her."

Conner watched him with those serious little eyes of his. Sometimes Kingsley felt as though his son was an old soul. It was impossible not to look into that innocent face and those eyes and not feel as though there was a lot more going on in there.

Conner nodded and then climbed onto his lap, hugging him. "Can't I go with you?"

Kingsley hugged his son tightly to him. "Not this time. Gabi can't come with me and neither can Mrs. Tillman."

He nodded. "Will you call me?"

"Yes. I will video chat with you anytime you want and every night before bed."

"Okay, you can go," Conner said.

"Thanks," he said. He wondered if, when he was little, he'd been as sure of himself and his place in the world as Conner was. He'd have to ask his older brother. His parents had been distant since he'd been arrested. His marriage and providing them a grandson had mollified them somewhat, but they still weren't sure he wasn't entirely blameless.

"You're awake," Gabi said from the doorway. "I thought we'd go down to the beach after your daddy leaves. Sound good?"

Conner nodded. "I have to potty."

He jumped off the bed and ran to his adjoining bathroom and Kingsley stood up and looked at Gabi. She watched him as though she didn't know what he was going to do next. He wasn't sure, either. He wanted to pull her into his arms.

Say to hell with everything else and carry her down to his bedroom. But he wasn't going to do that. When he'd been a quarterback he'd been known as the iceman. Nothing could shake him. And he channeled that right now.

He had to.

It was the only way he had been able to do what he'd had to on the field. Facing linebackers and rushers who wanted to punish the pretty boy who'd hurt a girl.

He had to put that in the past. Had to exonerate himself. Had to find a place where he could be the man he wanted to be for his son. And if he were being honest, for Gabi.

He wanted to get to know the woman she'd become without the big shadow of the past hanging over them.

"I'm not going to apologize."

"I wasn't about to ask you to. I'm still not sure what's going on between us."

"Good. I don't want to be managed by you. You'd probably draft up a plan like you advise parents to do and try to manage it."

She crossed her arms under her breasts and shook her head. "You're right. I want to deny it but I'm aching to plan this. To figure out what's going to happen next. But you won't let me."

"Good. You have become too rigid—too structured. You need a man to shake you up."

"I'm back," Conner announced. "And look what I did."

Kingsley turned to his son and noticed that he'd put on his swim trunks and swim shirt all by himself. He felt a lump in his throat. His little boy was getting so big.

"Good job," Gabi said. "High five."

She squatted down to Conner's level and held her hand up. He gave her a high five and then skipped over to Kingsley and smiled up at him.

Kingsley ruffled his son's hair. "I'll watch him while you change."

"Thanks."

Gabi left the room and when she returned a few minutes later, he wasn't disappointed. She had on pair of khaki shorts that ended midthigh, showing off her long, tanned legs, and a loose-fitting off-the-shoulder white top that revealed her bikini strap and her tanned shoulders.

He wanted to cancel his trip and stay with them. And he promised himself soon he'd be able to do just that. He said goodbye to Gabi and his son and left for the airport, in pursuit of answers to questions still lingering from the past.

Six

Gabi fell into a routine, and she soon learned that like every toddler, Conner had his temper tantrums when he was hungry or unable to get his point across to her. But on the whole, he was a good kid.

What unnerved her were some of the mannerisms she knew he shared with his father. Watching him eat a bowl of ice cream was like watching Kingsley do it. Then other times he would give her a look when she made him laugh that also reminded her of Kingsley.

She missed him.

Silly, she knew. But there it was. The house

was too big when he was gone. It had felt too small when he'd been there but now she realized it was his presence and not the house that was making her so aware of the space around her.

Kingsley video chatted with Conner every day at least once. Sometimes more. When she and Conner went for a walk on the beach and found an interesting piece of driftwood, Conner needed to send a picture to his dad and then talk to him. When Conner taught her how to play a racing video game, he wanted his dad to know. And every night after she finished reading him whatever book he'd chosen—his current favorite was *Good Night, Knight* after Gabi had told him she liked knights in shining armor—he had to call his dad and do their *One Fish Two Fish Red Fish Blue Fish* rap.

She knew that when the time came for her to go back to her house in Carmel and her regular life she was going to miss the little boy. But that didn't mean she was going to let his father walk all over her.

She and Conner had been to the beach, the park and had played video games but he didn't want to go to bed. She'd done all she could to get him ready but he wasn't having any of it.

She suspected it was because they hadn't been able to video chat with Kingsley all day. She got it—the kid missed his dad. She missed him, too, but he was in New York on business. And he'd warned them both that he might not be able to chat today.

"Let's try to call your dad one more time and then it's time for bed."

"Gammi, I can't sleep."

"You haven't tried."

"I just know I can't," he said with a big sigh.

"Your dad might answer," she said.

"I might get sleepy then."

She hoped so but she could tell by the way he watched her dial Kingsley's number from the iPad app that he was getting nervous.

She put her hand on his shoulder while they waited for Kingsley to answer. "Do you always get to see your daddy before bed?"

This was the first night they hadn't been able to talk to him.

"Yes," Conner said, nodding. He wrapped his

arms around himself and she stretched to reach his little stuffed pig and hand it to him. He pulled it close and kept staring at the screen.

Kingsley wasn't answering. On a hunch she hit the favorites button and noticed that Hunter was listed there.

"Would talking to Uncle Hunter help?" she asked.

Conner nodded. "Maybe he knows where Daddy is."

"Your daddy is fine. Remember he sent us that text around dinnertime? He said he'd be in a meeting until after your bedtime."

"I know. But maybe he got out early."

Gabi knew that men and women with demanding jobs couldn't pop out of meetings to talk to their kids. Intellectually that made perfect sense to her. So she could either text him that it was an emergency or come up with another distraction for Conner until Kingsley was out of his meeting.

"Want to roast marshmallows?"

"Yes! Like cowboys do when they are with the cows?"

"Just like the cattle drive," she said. They'd watched a video earlier that had depicted one.

She texted Kingsley to video call as soon as he was out of his meeting and helped Conner put his slippers on. He held his pig in one arm and the iPad in the other. She picked him up and carried him out to the patio area where there was a fire pit.

Mrs. Tillman had gone to bed in the guesthouse she lived in on the property, so it was just the two of them. In the distance she heard the winds blowing across the land and the sky was clear tonight.

"My cousin Gui used to tell me tales about the stars when I was little," she said as she sat Conner in one of the chairs, taking a thick blanket from the storage bench and wrapping it around him while she got the fire ready.

"Like what? Unca Hunter says a man lives in the moon."

"Did he? What does that man do up there?"

"He watches over me. My mommy asked him to," Conner said.

Gabi had a hard time reconciling the playboy

she knew Hunter to be with the man Conner knew. He was a good "uncle" to Conner and she could tell that Kingsley and he had each other's backs. That must be important to them both. After all, they were the only two people who knew what had really happened that night Stacia died.

She'd stopped thinking about it. Instead, she focused on her job of being a nanny to Conner and also trying really hard not to lust after Kingsley whenever he video chatted with his son.

But Kingsley had kissed her in a way that made it impossible to think of anything else. She'd wanted some peace of mind and hadn't even come close to finding it.

Not when he was here.

And certainly not when he was gone. It was as if…

What?

She liked him. She knew that. She wanted his body moving over hers—she admitted that, too. But another part of her, the woman who kept seeing signs of him in his son's face, wanted Kingsley to be something she thought she'd given up on wanting.

She wanted him to be her knight in shining armor. To woo her, and this time when he won her, to keep her.

Idiot.

She was too old to believe in fairy tales.

She got the fire started and they roasted marshmallows and told stories to each other until Conner drifted off to sleep. She kept his iPad open as she promised Conner she would and waited for a call from his father.

She finally acknowledged that Kingsley wasn't going to call and wondered what had distracted him from his son. She could think of only one thing. A woman.

She carried Conner to his bed and tucked him in before going to her own room, where she tossed and turned all night. She knew she had no claim on Kingsley. But she'd started to think he was someone else. A better man.

New York was too crowded and the party at the Kiwi Klub was too loud. Damn. He was getting old when he couldn't hang out in the club like he used to. But he was here with a purpose. Supposedly this was where he could find Daria Miller. She'd had her assistant text him the names of three different nightclubs she was checking out tonight.

"Kingsley Buchanan. I'm surprised you want to see me," she said, coming up next to him at the bar. She reached around him and took his drink—a scotch neat—and took a sip of it. "You know I'm a reporter, right?"

"That's precisely why I want to talk to you," he said, gesturing to the bartender for another drink.

Daria had short curly brown hair and a heart-shaped face. She was curvy and wore a pantsuit that accentuated her curves. Her eye makeup was understated and the look in her brown eyes was cautious.

"Finally decided to confess?" she asked.

"I already am on record with my story. I want to ask you about that night," he said. "What are you drinking?"

"Scotch," she said. "You really want to talk about that night?"

He ordered for her and when they each had their drinks he led the way to the VIP area. He found a quiet banquette toward the back of the roped-off area. Around them VIPs were partying but Kingsley wasn't interested in celebrity spotting. He wanted to know what Daria had experienced in college.

She sat down, crossing her legs. Her legs were nice enough but didn't hold his attention the way Gabi's did.

"What exactly do you want to talk about?"

"I read your blog post about people being drugged on college campuses and I wanted to know if anything like that went on at our school."

"Seriously?"

"Yeah. I know Hunter and I didn't harm Stacia, but someone did and I'm in a position now to find out who."

She leaned back against the bench and stared at him. He suspected it was her version of the truth stare. But he wasn't interested in lying about anything. He needed answers. And liars only heard more lies, in his experience.

"Convince me."

"Convince you? How about you just tell me what you know. I'm not really into talking people into believing me."

He'd missed talking to Conner and seeing Gabi to meet with Daria, and now it hardly seemed worth it. He put his glass down on the table and stood up. "Enjoy your drink."

"Kingsley, wait."

He turned around. She gestured to the seat he'd just vacated.

"Do you have something to tell me?" he asked. "I get that you might be curious given we went to the same school, but I'm not really here to satisfy that curiosity."

"I'll talk to you about what I know. Sit down," she said.

He did but left his drink on the table. He'd just ordered it out of habit. He wasn't really interested in drinking.

"I was surprised when you asked me about druggings on campus because your frat house was notorious for that behavior at parties. I know of at least seven women who went to parties there and woke up groggy the next morning with vague memories of sex and nothing else," she said.

"Date-rape drugs?" Kingsley asked. "I never knew anything about that. Did they have any idea who was involved?"

"I don't know. I wasn't working on the college paper back then. But I went through all the security records and found seven different girls over a four-year period."

"All the time Hunter and I were there?" he asked. He knew that he'd never drugged a girl. Since he was the star quarterback, panties had practically fallen off as he'd walked by women.

"Yes."

"Did the reports end when we left?" he asked.

She flushed and took a sip of her drink. "I never checked. I was determined to find out what really happened to Stacia, but the women who were drugged didn't run with you or Hunter so it was a dead end."

"Maybe it wasn't. What else did you uncover?" Hunter and he had both been over the night a million times, but there were pieces that were missing. Things they'd never been able to put together.

"You are serious about this," she said again. "I'm shocked. I thought you had moved on."

"The ID channel is running a ten-years-later special on the Frat House Murder. They always do those reenactments that make it seem like Hunter and I killed her. And I have son who's three, Daria. He's going to start school soon and the murder is always going to be a question in everyone's mind. But everyone still thinks I did it. Even you."

She leaned in and he had a feeling he was getting her reporter persona now. "Why? You have your life. You've been cleared of all charges."

"But everyone still thinks I did it. Even you."

She shook her head. "Touché. I think you might be changing my mind a bit."

"Would you mind sending me the research you did? I just want to see if there is something that you uncovered that will jog my memories of the night."

"If you uncover what happened, will you give me the story first?" she asked.

They would need someone to bring the story to light, and giving it to her wouldn't be a bad idea. "Sure."

"Okay. I'll send you what I have. It's not a lot. I mean, I copied the security reports and I have some videos and pictures that people took at the party that night."

"What were you going to do with them?" he asked.

"I'll compare them to see if the same people who were known to be at the other parties where the girls were drugged were there that night. There were no other reports of druggings the night Stacia died."

"Is that odd?" he asked. He couldn't wait to go through her notes.

"Sort of. Every other time it happened, there were a few women who reported feeling funny but who hadn't been attacked. Almost like the perpetrator had drugged a few women to see who would be an easy target."

"Interesting. I look forward to getting your

notes," he said, taking a business card out of his pocket and handing it to her. She took it from him, dropping it in her purse before she got to her feet and left.

He might have gotten their first solid lead on who had harmed Stacia. The campus security hadn't been cooperative when he'd called them and no one wanted to talk to the guy they thought was trying to pin his crime on someone else.

He pulled his phone from his pocket and noticed he'd missed several calls from Conner's iPad. He checked the time but it was too late to call. He texted his son to say he loved him and then texted Gabi to apologize.

Now that he was on the path to figuring out what had really happened, it didn't seem too far-fetched to think about the future and Gabi waiting for him at home. He knew he needed to call Conner but it was after two in the morning, which was eleven in Carmel. His son would be sleeping and he'd wait until the morning to call him.

* * *

Gabi woke to Kingsley's text message on her phone. She rolled over in bed and stared at it. She had about ten minutes before Conner woke up. Her habit was to always wake before her alarm went off. Even as a teenager she was always awake before it.

Kingsley's text wasn't very explanatory; in fact, it was almost impersonal. She hoped he sent something more to his son. Conner was going to want to talk to him as soon as he woke up.

She texted Kingsley back to that effect and he returned her text saying he was waiting for Conner to call him.

She hopped out of bed and hurried into the bathroom, taking a few minutes to pull her hair back so it didn't look so crazy. She debated putting on makeup but that would look as if she was trying to impress him. So she settled for a quick swipe of eyeliner to define her eyes and then went into Conner's room just as "Everything Is Awesome" started playing.

He rubbed his eyes and glanced over at her with his stuffed pig in his arms. His hair was tousled and his gaze moved from her to his iPad, which she'd left propped open on his nightstand.

"I have to potty," he said.

"Go ahead, I'll keep my eye on the iPad."

He ran into the bathroom and then came back out a few minutes later. Just as he sat down on his bed again and was opening the app to video chat with his dad, Kingsley called him.

Conner hit the button and stared down at his dad's face. Happiness lit up the little boy's face. "Daddy, we missed you last night."

"I know, buddy. I'm so sorry. Tell me what you did yesterday."

As Conner talked, Gabi stared at Kingsley. It was just after noon on the East Coast. She was trying to see if he was in a hotel room but soon realized that he was in a car.

"Gammi didn't know about the man in the moon," Conner was saying. "But she did know some camping songs."

"That's good. So you enjoyed the campfire and then told her about the man in the moon. What else?"

"I fell asleep waiting for you. Was your meeting good?" Conner asked.

"It was. I might be done early."

"Yippee!" Conner jumped up on his bed and danced around on it. "Daddy is coming home!"

"Not yet, buddy. I'm trying to set up one more meeting before I can get back. I'll let you know at bedtime tonight."

"Okay. Love you, Daddy."

"Love you, too, Con. Go brush your teeth so I can talk adult stuff with Gabi."

"Okay."

Conner scampered off, his energy palpable now that he'd talked to his dad.

"What's up? Also, what kind of meeting were you at so late at night? Conner goes to bed at eight," she said.

"I wanted to let you know that I'm going to be leaving Manhattan and heading to Chicago. I will text you when my meeting's over," he said.

She noticed he didn't say what kind of meeting it was.

She felt a little angry because now she thought it might have been a date. And she knew she had no reason to be angry. They'd kissed—that was it. That wasn't a promise of anything except maybe another kiss. But Conner had been really upset that his father hadn't called last night.

"You know, it's fine if you want to go on a date. But Conner was worried about you. I almost called Hunter to calm him down. He wouldn't go to sleep."

"If it was a date, Gabriella, I would have said it was a date. I wouldn't have called it a meeting. I didn't mean to worry him. When Jade died in the car accident, he was too young to remember. He only knows that she was traveling. This hasn't been an issue before. I'll talk with him when I'm home," Kingsley said.

Gabi didn't feel that bad about assuming he was on a date. She knew lots of parents who claimed to be in meetings when they weren't. "I can help, too. We are going to be here all day today. We didn't discuss this, but how do you feel about me conducting meetings out of the home office?"

He rubbed the back of his neck. He looked

tired and stressed now that she was really looking at him.

"I'd rather you didn't. I haven't advertised my address because there are people who post that information about me and Hunter on the web."

She had heard of those websites, had even stumbled on one when she'd done her Google search. He was listed on a blog run by someone named Captain Justice called *Presumed Guilty as Hell*. It had struck her as ironic that the blogger posted personal information about suspects who'd been wrongly accused but kept his own identity hidden.

"No problem. I'm still trying to figure out the logistics of working from here. A week isn't a long time."

"Wow, it's already been a week," he said. "Are you glad I blackmailed you into helping me out?"

"Glad? No, not really. But I do like this job and it's giving me a lot of ideas for my column," she said, smiling.

"I'm glad to hear that. Is there anything else I need to know?"

"I'm scheduled for a talk at a women's group

a week from Thursday. Will you be back by then?" she asked.

"I will. I expect to be home either later tomorrow or the day after," he said.

"Conner will be happy to hear it," she said.

A minute later he was back in his bedroom. She scooted over so he could hold the iPad and talk to Kingsley again.

Conner leaned in close to the camera and gave his dad a big smile. "How's my teeth?"

Gabi had to laugh. She wondered how much of last night's upset had to do with being tired, because he was fine today.

"Perfect. See you soon," Kingsley said.

"Bye, Daddy," Conner replied, disconnecting the call.

She spent the rest of the morning trying to forget that moment when Kingsley had said he wasn't on a date. It didn't mean anything.

And during Conner's nap, when she came across pictures of him in a club on a society blog, she realized it really didn't mean anything. Except he'd lied.

Seven

"So this place is nice," Melissa said as she put a stack of papers in front of Gabi to sign the next day. "Doesn't seem like it's much of a hardship to be living here. I think I'd spend all day staring out the window."

Gabi smiled at her assistant. "Did I make the wrong choice when I promoted you?"

"Hell, no. Just saying. You weren't too sure about working here—"

"Not because of the location. Who wouldn't want to be on a cliff-top mansion with the Pacific Ocean stretching endlessly in front of them?"

"So how is the kid? Is he spoiled?"

Gabi shook her head. She turned away from Melissa, thinking about how sweet little Conner was. He was the kind of child that made being a nanny easy. She loved his attitude and the way he was well behaved. She tried to ignore the fact that a lot of that had to do with Kingsley. Conner had his moments when he went into toddler meltdown, but King was firm with him. She'd seen the way he handled Conner's temper. He made sure Conner knew his behavior wasn't acceptable and always got him back on track.

She was impressed.

Not just with the three-year-old. But also with his thirtysomething father. Kingsley might have come back to California for reasons he wasn't being entirely clear with her on, but a part of her was starting to believe him when he'd said it was because he wanted Conner to have all the advantages of growing up in the sun and sand that Kingsley hadn't had.

"Conner is great. It's just that I haven't nannied in so long and I'm busy with the admin stuff. Thanks for driving out here today to deliver this paperwork. I'm glad we got the visas for South America out of the way. We also need to have proof of vaccinations before any of our employees leave for the rain forest."

"I'm on it," Melissa said. "I need some advice on something."

"Shoot."

"Abby is back. She wants to try another placement. I feel like she's taking advantage of our friendship," Melissa said.

Abby wasn't the best nanny; she flirted with a lot of the fathers so the moms weren't exactly keen to have her living in. "What did she say?"

"Just that she really needs a job and since I was in charge of hiring…"

"She can't go back into a house, but have you considered her as your assistant?" Gabi suggested. Gabi had a soft spot for Abby. She was a hard worker, and the kids loved her. And Gabi hated to think of anyone who was willing to work not working.

"I hadn't. That's a good idea. I will mention it to her," Melissa said. "Thanks."

"No problem. I get how hard it is to deal with friends and business."

"Wasn't that how you got started?" Melissa asked.

"Yes, Mal knew my parents. So when he mentioned needing a nanny…my mom said I would do it."

"What? She didn't even ask you?"

"Nope. She just decided I'd been figuring out my next move long enough and she pushed me back out into the world."

"That's funny. Were you mad?"

"At first, but it turned out to be the best thing for me. It gave me a chance to find a career I wouldn't have ever thought to try. And now it's a big business. I'd never admit it to her, but she's always known best."

"Moms are like that."

"They are. I think I've signed everything. I have a meeting tomorrow with the city planners about the playground that Kingsley's funding. I'm not sure if he will be back. If not, would you watch Conner while I go to the meeting? The housekeeper has a dentist appointment tomorrow."

"No problem. In fact, I don't have to be back

to the office until two. Want me to meet him today?" Melissa asked.

"Yes, let's go."

Melissa put all the paperwork that Gabi had signed into her big leather backpack and they went down the hall to the sunny nursery where Conner was playing with his Duplo and Lego blocks. Mrs. Tillman was sitting on a chair in the sun reading on her Kindle.

"I guess my break is over," she said with a wink.

"Mrs. Tillman, this is my assistant, Melissa." The two women shook hands and chatted while Gabi went over to check on Conner.

"What are you building?"

"A space station," he said. "Want to help?"

"Sure. I brought Melissa in to meet you. She's going to watch you tomorrow while I'm at a meeting," Gabi said.

Conner looked up at Melissa, who'd finished talking to Mrs. Tillman and had joined them. She squatted down next to Conner.

"Hey, kiddo."

"Hello."

"Can I help with the space station? I went to space camp when I was a teenager. So I know a few things that they don't show everyone."

"Cool. Like what?"

Melissa showed him how to build an observation platform and Gabi stood up to straighten the room, surprised when she noticed that Kingsley stood in the doorway. He was back early.

"Daddy!" Conner yelled and jumped up to run over to his father.

Kingsley picked Conner up and hugged him tightly, kissing the top of his head.

"How have you been?"

"Great. I'm building a space station."

"I see that," Kingsley said.

"Will you be okay with Conner while Gabi and I speak in the other room?" Kingsley asked Melissa.

Gabi realized as he turned back to her and gestured for her to precede him out of the room that Kingsley was pissed. She could see it in his eyes. She wasn't sure what had happened.

She led the way down the hall to his home office and stepped inside. The shutters hadn't been opened and the room was dark and cold as she walked into it.

She didn't want to be alone with him now that she realized he hadn't been honest with her. She wished she could say that his lying to her would be enough to make her not want to kiss him and run her hands all over him, but that wasn't the case. He looked tired. As though his trip hadn't been a good one. She wanted to ignore what she'd seen, what she'd found out with a little internet digging and just open her arms to him.

Offer him comfort and whatever else he wanted.

Damn.

She was weak where he was concerned. She always had been and that was her problem. No matter how many times she thought she'd moved on, as soon as they were in the same room she was ready to believe whatever he said.

But she needed answers. And she wasn't going to be pacified by any half-truths. After first thinking he'd been on a date with the woman he'd been photographed with on the society blog, she'd remembered something. The woman looked familiar. So Gabi had done more research. She'd uncovered some things on the internet that led her to believe that Kingsley and Hunter might be back in California for, well, revenge.

And she had admitted to herself she simply didn't know him well enough to rule that out as a possibility. But she knew that if she'd been wronged the way they had...well, she would be tempted to find out who had set her up and then get back at the person, too.

"What the hell is she doing here?" Kingsley said. "I thought I was clear that for what I was paying, you were to be Conner's nanny."

Gabi turned to face him. "Watch your tone, Kingsley. Melissa had to deliver some papers for my signature and since I have a meeting tomorrow that I can't miss and you weren't supposed to be back, she was getting to know Conner so that when she watched him at my office tomorrow he'd feel more comfortable."

He looked chagrined for a second, pushing his hand through his thick hair. He shook his head. "Sit down, Gabi. Let's be civilized."

"Why wouldn't we be?" she asked. "It's not like one of us is here for revenge."

"What did you say?" He stood up and walked around his desk toward her but she stood her ground.

"Just playing a hunch. Looks like I hit pay dirt," she said. "I thought that woman in the photo with you on the society blog looked familiar. She went to school with us. She was in my humanities class."

"What's that got to do with revenge?" he asked. His voice was low and controlled.

"Nothing on the surface. But she contacted me about four years ago and asked me what I remembered of the party that night. Had I felt drugged or anything."

Kingsley turned away from her and paced over to the window. "I didn't see your name in the file she gave me."

"Probably because I wasn't drugged and I didn't drink anything. I was focused on you. I didn't want to have any hazy memories or anything like that. I knew our night together was one I wanted to remember," she said. Saying it out loud reminded her that it was true. She'd thought she and Kingsley were special. She'd believed in happily-ever-after.

"I'm sorry. I wish I could have given you everything you dreamed of instead of having you wake up to that nightmare. I'm trying to make things right. Hunter and I heard some stories over the last few years of incidents that were similar to what happened to Stacia. We know we didn't do anything like that, so we're investigating. It isn't *revenge*."

Gabi closed the gap between them and put her hand right in the middle of his chest. His heartbeat was solid under her palm and he smelled good. That expensive cologne of his always made her want to curl up in his arms.

"I know you, Kingsley. You aren't someone who's going to be content to say, 'We found the guy who did this.' You and I both know that. Be honest with me."

He looked down at her, his eyes so cold and icy that she dropped her hand from his chest. Oh, yes, he was here for revenge. He was here to ruin whoever had crossed him all those years ago and set him up to take the fall for something he hadn't done.

* * *

Revenge. When she said it he didn't like the way it sounded. But he wasn't going to be swayed from his path, not now.

"You're right. I do want to find out what happened and make sure the one responsible pays," he said. "But that has nothing to do with you."

He took her hand and put it back on his chest. He liked it when she touched him. He was tired. Frustrated from all the dead ends he'd chased. Talking to women who thought he was guilty and had bought his freedom had left him with a sour taste in his mouth.

He'd gone to Chicago to speak with two of the women mentioned in Daria's files, but they hadn't wanted to speak to him. He couldn't blame them.

He had no idea how he was going to make any inroads with his investigation. He'd reviewed the videos Daria had supplied, but most of them were shaky and he hadn't seen anything new. The pictures were also a dead end. He'd sent everything to Hunter to review, as well. But in terms of interviewing the women who'd been drugged, he doubted Hunter was going to get a warmer reception than he had, so they were stuck.

And vengeance and justice seemed even further away today than it had last week.

His body said the only thing that would relieve the stress and pain was Gabi. But he also didn't feel right kissing her. He felt tainted by the past and though nothing—absolutely freakin' nothing—had changed, it felt as if it had.

He lowered his head slowly, giving her time to pull away, but she went on her tiptoes, her hand pushing against his chest as their lips met.

This kiss wasn't the carnal dare the last one had been. This was all Gabi. She was the gentle breeze that circled his home on a spring day, thawing those frozen, broken parts of his soul that he'd always pretended didn't exist.

He knew he shouldn't do this. Any more than he should have kept dating her when she'd come to see him in jail. Right now, by asking questions, he was stirring up things people had forgotten about.

She bit his lower lip. Surprised, he drew his head back.

"What was that for?"

"For not paying attention to the kiss. What's distracting you?" she asked.

"I shouldn't do this. Before I started asking questions I felt like you and I could have an affair and there wouldn't be any repercussions, but now...I'm not so sure," he admitted.

He wasn't afraid to let her see the real man behind the confident swagger.

Gabi had always been the one person he felt he could let his guard down with.

"Let me be the judge of what's right for me. I'm a big girl now," she said.

But being a big girl had nothing to do with the ugly gossip that could come from nowhere. Even his wife had been painted with some ugly innuendo after they'd married. Jade hadn't allowed it to bother her, but she'd been used to ignoring the paparazzi and Gabi wasn't.

Gabi was a nanny who had spent most of her adult life taking care of wealthy children. There was nothing that would have prepared her—

"Stop it."

"Stop what?"

"Trying to tell yourself that I need you to protect me. I've gotten along just fine without you. I want you to see me as a woman. Not someone fragile creature you have to protect."

"I always see you as a woman," he replied. "In fact, it's been damn hard to see you any other way. Every night when I saw Conner on the video chat I couldn't help staring at you when he wasn't looking. I think I'm obsessed."

"Obsession isn't necessarily a bad thing," she said. "But I'm not an object you are watching from afar. I'm right here with you, and instead of talking about revenge and the past, how about we do something about it?"

"What did you have in mind?" he asked. Revenge was slowly being pushed to the back of his mind.

She eased her hands under his sport coat and slowly worked it off his shoulders and down his arms. He let it slide to the floor and then stood there waiting to see what she'd do next.

He liked Gabi like this. When she took control.

She went up on her tiptoes and twined her

hands around the back of his neck. "Now, let's try this welcome-home kiss thing again."

"Oh, it was a welcome-home kiss?" he asked. Her breath was minty fresh and brushed over his lips when she talked. Her curvy petite body was pressed against his chest, and her fingers were fondling the back of his neck.

Shivers spread down his spine and he was suddenly very aware of every second since the last time he'd held this woman in his arms. He wanted her.

Blood pooled in his groin and his erection grew. He lowered his head slowly and this time thought of nothing but her full mouth and how she tasted when he kissed her.

She parted her lips under his, her tongue sliding deep into his mouth. He put his hands on her waist and drew her closer, rubbing his groin against her center. A soft little moan escaped her.

He was on fire.

He lifted her off her feet and turned to walk to his desk. He set her down on the edge of it without breaking the kiss and stepped between her legs. Now that she was seated on his desk, he was free to let his hands roam all over her. He caressed her back, squeezing her hips as he drew her even closer to his erection, rubbing against her as she deepened the kiss.

Her fingers tangled in the hair at the back of his neck and tugged as she bit lightly at his tongue.

He knew that he was going to have to stop soon. His son was just down the hall along with two women in their employ. This wasn't proper behavior—but he knew he'd never really given a crap about proper behavior.

And he certainly wasn't going to start now when he had Gabi in his arms and she was setting him on fire.

There was a knock at the door and he tore his mouth from hers.

"Who is it?"

"Mrs. Tillman. Sorry to interrupt, but Hunter is here and he says he needs to speak to you urgently."

"Kingsley—for God's sake, Mrs. Tillman, let me by," Hunter said through the door. Kingsley wasn't going to pull away from Gabi like an embarrassed lothario, but he didn't want Hunter to say anything rude.

"Just a minute, Hunter."

He kissed Gabi again softly. "Dinner tonight after Conner is in bed."

She nodded. He helped her off his desk and she walked out of his office past a stunned Hunter and a smiling Mrs. Tillman.

Eight

Driving from Kingsley's coastal mansion into Carmel wasn't a burden. The day was beautiful and she felt so good and happy.

Kingsley was back in town.

So different from how she'd felt when he'd walked in her door. A part of her was afraid to trust the way she felt about him. This was Kingsley Buchanan and he lived life on his own terms. Even before he'd been arrested he'd been his own man.

But this time...she couldn't help it. She was falling in love with him again. She knew it.

There was nothing else to explain why she kept

grinning. And when she gathered her notes to go into the meeting with the community leaders, she couldn't help the feeling of pride that Kingsley was the man who was making this new playground possible.

Her phone rang as she was about to get out of the car. A glance at the caller ID showed it was her mom.

"Hi, Mom."

"Gabi, hello. You haven't called me in days. I was worried about you."

"Why were you worried?" she asked. "I told you I was working as a nanny in a client's home and that I would check in when I could. And I did text you last night."

"Texting doesn't put my mind at ease. Someone else could have your phone and send that." Gabi laughed and her mom started laughing, too. "Okay, so maybe I worry too much."

"You do," Gabi told her. "Why are you calling?"

"Are you free for brunch on Sunday? Your brother is in town and wants us to meet his girlfriend."

"Definitely. I want to meet her. Alejandro has been too secretive about her. I'm curious," Gabi said. "I might bring a date."

"Really? Both of my kids with a date. I won't be able to eat from all the excitement."

"Is that sarcasm? You'd think someone who was worried I might be in danger would be a bit nicer," Gabi said.

"Ha. Who's your mystery man?" her mom asked.

Gabi bit her lip. "Kingsley Buchanan."

"Kingsley? The boy from college? Gabi, now I really am worried."

"Mom, don't be. It's not like I thought."

"What about how I thought? That we were lucky you weren't dead, too."

"Mom! He was cleared of any charges."

"But no one knows what really happened."

"Kingsley does and he said he didn't do it," Gabi said.

Then she realized how that sounded. As though she was grasping at straws to convince her mom of Kingsley's innocence. But she did believe him and she always had. But if her mom was this hard to convince, her father would be even harder. "Never mind. I'll come alone."

"Gabi, I'm sorry, but I just want what's best for you," her mom said.

"I know that. I have a meeting, so I better let you go," Gabi said.

"Not yet. Tell me why you like this—why you like Kingsley."

Why did she like him? It was always hard to put feelings into words and she worried that she'd sound like an idiot. But she closed her eyes and thought of Kingsley. Of how he'd looked when he came home from being on the road doing business.

"He makes me laugh, Mom. And he's smart and a good dad. His little boy is sweet and charming—a mini version of Kingsley."

"He has a son?"

"Yes. Mom, everyone knows he has a son. He also is a famous sports agent now that he's quit playing football."

"Oh, I didn't follow him after he left your life."

Gabi understood that. Her mom didn't dwell on the past—she was more of a shake-it-off-and-move-on type of person. "He's trying to move on for his son. And there are a lot of things about that night that make no sense. I think that's why the DA dropped the charges."

"Okay. I will talk to your father, but we'd love to have you and Kingsley and his son for brunch on Sunday."

She realized that her mom was going to be fair and give Kingsley a chance. For her. That meant a lot. "I'll have to ask Kingsley."

"Okay. Let me know. Call me later and I'll tell you what I've found out about Alejandro's girl-friend."

"I will," she said.

She hung up the phone and fiddled with her notes one more time before texting Kingsley.

Would you like to go to brunch on Sunday at my parents' house?

Do they know you are bringing me?

Duh. I asked if you wanted to go.

Conner too?

Yes.

Sure, as long as they are civil about the past.

They will be.

She typed in her next message and hesitated before finally hitting Send.

It never goes away, does it? You constantly have to deal with that night.

I am. That's why I want to put it to rest once and for all.

I can help.

I appreciate that. But I don't want you involved.

We can talk later. I'm off to my meeting now.

Gabi, I mean it. I don't want this to taint you at all.

Bye. See you at home later.

She wasn't going to let Kingsley tell her what to do. The affection she had for him was still growing inside her. When she thought of Conner and Kingsley she didn't want the two of them to continue to live with the aftermath of false accusations. She knew it was going to be hard. But she wanted to help Kingsley figure what happened so he could move on to a future with her.

"Go long," Kingsley said, and Hunter ran a pattern they'd done a million times before. Kingsley threw the ball and a few seconds later Hunter leaped in the air, caught it and started running, only to be blocked by Conner, who launched himself at Hunter's knees and brought him down.

Hunter rolled carefully, scooping up Conner with him so that he didn't hurt the toddler, and then sat up.

"I got you," Conner said.

"You sure did. You're pretty good at this. Thinking about being a football player someday like your daddy and me?"

Conner shook his head. "I'm going to be a knight."

"Wow, really? There aren't that many knights around these days," Hunter said.

"Gammi likes them," Conner said. "Daddy, I can be a knight, right?"

Gabi liked knights. Who knew? He was going to have to look into that a bit more. She seemed way too practical and too much of a twenty-first-century independent woman.

"You sure can," he said. "Modern knights are men who are polite and always treat a woman like a lady."

Hunter snorted. "Good luck with that."

"Thanks!" Conner said with a big grin.

Conner stole the ball from Hunter, jumped off him and ran the ball back to Kingsley.

"Want to try to catch it this time?" Kingsley asked his son.

"Yes," Conner said.

"Come here and I'll show you how to run the pattern," Hunter said.

Conner jogged back to Hunter and Kingsley watched his best friend and his son. Hunter would be a good father if given the chance. But not as long as the specter of Stacia's death hung over them both.

He had no idea what they would find next. He

knew they were going to need some help. Most of the women who'd been drugged at the parties in college weren't interested in talking to him or Hunter. He toyed with asking Gabi to reach out to them. It would be the simplest thing. But he didn't really want her involved in the matter.

"You going to throw the ball or just stare at us?" Hunter asked.

He tossed the ball to Conner, careful to throw where he knew his son would be. He also didn't put the same force he would put behind a throw for Hunter. His son caught it and Kingsley felt a wave of love wash over him at the pure joy on Conner's face.

"Daddy, I did it."

"You sure did."

They played until the sun started to set. Hunter and he drank beers while they watched Conner playing with his toy set on the living room floor.

"I saw that Gabi is the head of the alumni committee," Hunter said.

"I noticed that, too. I'm not sure how that will help us," Kingsley said. They both were talking quietly. Conner seemed engrossed in his play, but Kingsley didn't want to take a chance on saying anything that his son would repeat later.

"Me, either. Just mentioning it. I have been over the files you sent me. I noticed that Mitch's name was in there a lot."

"You keep in touch with him?" Kingsley asked. Mitch had been a defensive back on the college team. And Kingsley hadn't really ever had a chance to talk to the man. Maybe once or twice but for the most part he was a stranger.

"No. But I think that Chuck has. I am going to take my Harley and drive over to the college and see if he will talk to me," Hunter said. "Want to come with me?"

Chuck had been a running back and now coached special teams for their former college. Kingsley and he had both played for New York, so he knew Chuck pretty well. "I might. I can't go on a bike if we take Conner with us."

"I was thinking that your nanny would be back by now," Hunter said.

"Well, she's meeting with the town council today. I think the meeting is going to go long," he said. "How about if we plan for tomorrow?

Maybe we can drop by our coach's house, as well. His housekeeper might know when he's going to be back home."

"Good thinking," Hunter said. "I wasn't able to find out why he was in the hospital. But he is getting old. It's odd to think of the man who was such a tyrant on the field being sick."

"It is," Kingsley agreed. Coach Gainer had always been tough but fair. He had worked them hard every day they were on campus and it had paid off. He'd never resented those long grueling hours since they had brought him the results he'd wanted.

"Maybe we can get Gabi to help," Hunter said.

"I really don't want her involved in this," Kingsley said.

"Involved in what?" Hunter asked. "Women will talk to her. They aren't going to talk to us."

"That's precisely what I don't want her involved in," Kingsley said.

"Involved in what?" Gabi said from the doorway, surprising them both.

"Our investigation," Hunter said.

"Hunter, don't—"

Hunter was determined to ignore his wishes on this and that pissed him off. Gabi wasn't a pawn to be used by either of them.

"It's okay," Gabi said. "What can I do?"

"Nothing. As soon as you start asking questions, people are going to think you know more about that night," Kingsley said. "You can't have that. Your business will suffer."

Hunter didn't look happy but then he nodded. "King is right. Sorry, Gabi. I wasn't thinking about how this will look to your clients if you start asking questions on our behalf."

"It's okay. I have drinks with a group from my sorority once a month. I can ask if anyone remembers hearing stories from that night. I'll say that you are back in town and that's what made me think of it."

"Won't they talk?" Kingsley asked. Every instinct he had said she should stay away from questioning anyone.

"Not my girls. We're solid. And we're sisters. I'm happy to do it. Also, I could contact the women on your list, Kingsley, for an article for the alumni newsletter."

Kingsley didn't like it. He wanted vengeance on the person who had framed them, and that was something that was too...too dark for Gabi. He didn't want any of this to touch her, but as they looked through the new photos King had found together he realized it already had.

He had come back to fix this for himself but he realized now he had to fix the past for Gabi, too.

Gabi hadn't been on a date in about six months. It wasn't that she didn't like going out. It was simply...well, if Melissa and her mother were to be believed, she was too picky.

Picky.

That made it sound as if she had hordes of great guys to choose from, but the truth was she didn't meet that many men who were interested in her. Most guys her age were married or in serious relationships. And then the fact that she owned a nanny service made the men she did meet fear she wanted kids right away.

So it was slim pickings, as her dad used to say.

But none of that explained why she'd taken extra care with her makeup and hair after she'd put Conner to bed. Or the fact that she'd ordered a new dress from Nordstrom and paid Melissa double time to pick it up and bring it to her at Kingsley's house.

She knew the truth. She hated to admit it even to herself, but it was staring back at her in the mirror. She wanted this date to be a good one. She wanted the past mistakes between her and Kingsley to fade away. She wanted this to be some kind of over-the-top romantic date that she could use to replace the memories of their first one. A frat party that had ended in murder.

Damn.

She realized that all of her dreams of the future had changed that night. She had wanted a family. She had wanted to find what her parents had found when they were young. A partner. Someone to share her life with. She was staring down thirty. Honestly, by this time she'd imagined she'd have a family of her own. Not still be taking care of other families.

But none of that mattered tonight. Tonight was just a date.

Yes, her first in a while. Yes, one with Kingsley Buchanan. Yes, she wanted it to be perfect.

But she had that tingling in her stomach that warned her she was already in over her head. Heck, she'd known that when she'd defended Kingsley to her mother. When she'd come up with excuses as to why he'd been at a nightclub with another woman. When she'd carefully worded the proposal to the county commissioners so that Kingsley's name wasn't in it.

She was hedging her bets. Being careful to be on her best behavior. And it seemed that Kingsley was doing the same.

They were both pretending.

She knew it. She wondered if he did.

It would be so easy to pretend she wasn't. But she knew herself. She wouldn't lie; Kingsley was the one man she'd always had regrets about. The one man that she wanted a proper resolution with.

But she was afraid to trust in Kingsley and his real reasons for wanting her. Oh, she didn't doubt the power of the attraction between them.

What she wasn't sure about was whether or not he'd still want her after she slept with him.

She put her lipstick down, braced her hands on the marble countertop and looked into the mirror.

There it was in her eyes. The secret fear that she'd been hiding and ignoring for too long— she was afraid to sleep with him in case it was like the last time when one night was all he spent with her.

She'd been cautious in her intimate relationships, always picking men who were staid and sensible. They weren't the most passionate of men, but they were consistent. But King wasn't. And he never had been.

He'd been the handsome, popular guy on campus and despite everything life had thrown at him, he still was. And it wasn't that she doubted her ability to keep his attention. She knew he liked her and had confidence in herself. It was just that the last time they'd slept together everything had changed between them. She'd be a fool to think this time would be any different.

Before she'd been a girl—no matter how mature she thought she was, she'd been a little bit silly and a lot foolish. But this time she was smarter.

Or at least she hoped she was.

Though already she liked him. And that was really too weak a word to describe what she felt for him. She knew seeing him with Conner had weakened her resolve. Hearing him talk passionately about needing to put the past to rest so that he could move on had made her dream that he'd move on with her.

But the truth was she was integral to the past. He needed her thoughts on—

"Stop it."

She spoke out loud to quiet her mind. Straightening her shoulders, she fiddled with her hair, put on her lipstick and walked away from the mirror and the woman in it who was afraid.

Six months. It didn't seem that long to be without a date until tonight.

She realized that her nerves had nothing to do with King or his intentions and everything to do with herself. She hadn't dated because she was tired of going through the routine of being someone she wasn't in the hopes that some guy would see through the ruse and like the real woman underneath.

So tonight…

Tonight she wasn't going to do it. She had nothing to lose with King. She knew that. The odds were already stacked against them really being anything other than lovers. She was going to be herself and if he didn't like it…well, that was too bad for him.

Because she couldn't change any more than she already had.

And she liked the woman she was. She forgot that sometimes when she was working, writing, mentoring Melissa. But she truly liked the woman she'd become over the years. The woman that the one night she'd spent with Kingsley had started her on the journey to becoming.

She opened her hall door and walked toward the dining room. When she got there a single rose waited on the table with a small note card with instructions to go to the patio.

She sniffed the rose as she felt that tingle of excitement in her stomach once again.

Candlelight flickered on the patio and flames danced in the large outdoor fire pit. When she stepped outside, her heel caught and she started to stumble, but King was there.

He caught her and she looked up into his eyes. "I've got you."

He definitely did.

Nine

Kingsley had spent a good deal of time over the years thinking about this night. He'd never really imagined it would happen, but he'd always wanted it to. He wanted to make up to Gabi for all the mistakes he'd made. He'd been young and selfish the first time he'd taken her to his bed. He'd done his best to make it pleasurable for her but she'd always been the one woman to set fire to his veins. A fire that burned straight through his self-control.

Holding her in his arms reminded him that she still had that power.

"Now that you've got me, what are you going

to do with me?" she asked. Her words were light but her tone was serious. She was nervous.

"Keep you safe," he said. But he was afraid that might be a promise he couldn't keep. Men focused on revenge had to be aware that there would be collateral damage.

"Promise?"

"Yes."

He knew he shouldn't have said that, but he couldn't help himself. He wanted to protect her.

She opened her mouth but he kissed her before she could ask for more promises from him. He didn't want to talk. Not about this. Not about anything serious. He wanted tonight to be something out of a dream.

He knew from Conner that she liked white knights. Men in shining armor who rode to the rescue of their woman. Damned if he wasn't a battered warrior in severely tarnished armor, but he still wanted to be her hero.

Her mouth was soft and she tasted of fresh mint and something else that was just Gabi. He took his time because it was a mellow California evening and he wanted it to last forever.

He wanted this night to be the start of something new between them. A beginning where he didn't let her down and she began to see him as…well, her hero.

He tangled one hand in her thick hair and let the cool, silky tresses play through his fingers. She tipped her head back and he thrust his tongue deeper into her mouth. She moved in his arms, her body undulating against his.

He put his other hand on her hip and drew her closer, wrapped his fingers around her and squeezed. She moaned and he felt everything inside his body clench. He lifted his head and looked down into her dark brown eyes. He saw the hope and the fear in them and realized that this night was more important than he could have ever imagined.

That tonight he was either going to make up for the past and start a new future with Gabi or he was going to put her forever out of his reach.

He knew what he wanted to happen.

He also had enough experience to know when he wanted something or someone this badly he often made mistakes.

He rubbed his thumb over her lower lip. God, he loved her mouth. It was full and lush and really he could spend all day kissing her. "Ready for a night to remember?"

"I am," she said.

He linked their fingers together and led her to the seating area in front of the fire pit. Mrs. Tillman had made them some appetizers and he had a pitcher of margaritas for them to share.

He seated her and felt the cool evening breeze. Gabi wore a sleeveless sheath made of white lace that showed off her tanned skin. He reached for the package he had placed underneath the bench before she got there and handed it to her as he sat down.

"What? You didn't have to get me anything," she said.

"I know. But I saw this while I was in New York and it reminded me of you," he said.

She gave him a sweet smile. "This is the first gift you've given me."

He knew that, as well. They hadn't dated long enough before his arrest for birthdays or holidays. He'd never had the chance to know if she was a slow present unwrapper or one of those who tore the paper off. Little things that seemed inconsequential until he found the right person.

Damn. This was a date. *Just a date*, he reminded himself.

Gabi was here. She was hot. And he had a lot to make up for from the past. That was it.

She carefully untied the blue ribbon and put it around her neck. His eyes followed the movement, noticing how long her neck was. He reached over to tuck her hair back behind her shoulder, pretending it was so he could see the ribbon better, knowing it was because he needed to touch her.

"Very pretty."

"Thank you," she said. "I love ribbons."

He'd had no idea. But he would remember it for the future.

She carefully unwrapped the box and set the paper aside once she'd folded it. She held the box on her lap, running her fingers over the Bergdorf Goodman lettering before slowly opening it.

Beneath the tissue was the scarf he'd picked out. It was multicolored and had crystals woven into it in a pattern. She pulled it out and held it up in front of her. Then she put it on her lap and traced the gems with her fingers.

"Thank you so much. It's gorgeous."

She stood up after setting the box to the side and put the scarf around her shoulders. She turned and glanced back at him over her shoulder.

"How do I look?"

"Beautiful," he said. His voice sounded hoarse and he knew that was because all the blood in his body had raced to his groin. He was hot and hard. Ready for her.

But when she smiled sweetly at him, he knew he could wait. Just barely.

This night had the promise of being more than sex. Of having all the romance that they had never experienced together.

He took the remote for the Bose speaker out of his pocket and hit Play. The sultry sounds of blues guitar filled the patio and he walked over to Gabi.

"Dance?"

She nodded. He pulled her into his arms and

danced her around the patio under the stars. And though he knew he'd done this all for her, he felt himself falling under a spell. He wanted to pretend that it was the trappings or romance that were making his heart beat faster, but he knew that was a lie.

It was the girl… Gabi was the one responsible.

The music changed from slow blues to "Smooth" by Santana and Rob Thomas. She'd loved that song when they'd been in college. Rob Thomas had been her first teenage crush. And she was pretty sure she'd mentioned it to Kingsley.

She tipped her head back and smiled up at him. "I like this song."

"I remember. You played it for me and made me listen to the lyrics."

"God, I was so annoying back then," she said. "Seriously, what was I thinking?"

"This song meant something to you," he said. "I did listen to the lyrics, and not just because kissing you made me hotter than I'd ever been in my life."

"That's saying something," she said with a small smile. "Why are you romancing me tonight?"

"I like you," he said simply.

"I like you, too," she said. "But that's not enough to warrant all of this."

"Why do you think I'm doing it?" he asked.

She studied him in the light from the flickering candles. His face was serene and as usual he gave away nothing that he was feeling. In fact, the only time she'd seen real emotion on his face was when he looked at Conner. Then she saw alpha dad in his eyes. Now, though, she wanted to see affection and maybe a little devotion, but she didn't see anything.

"I don't know," she said, pulling the gem-encrusted scarf closer around her shoulders as she stepped back from him. "You've got every detail planned, don't you?"

He shrugged and turned to the pitcher of margaritas, pouring each of them a glass. She took one from him.

"To old friends."

Old friends? That wasn't what they were.

Maybe she'd been taken in by the house and the kid. Maybe she was pretending there was something more between Kingsley and her. Or was she?

"I'm so unsure tonight," she said. "That's not like me. I don't know if it's the past making me feel this way or you."

He set his drink on the table and came over to her. He took her glass and placed it next to his. Then he wrapped his arms around her and held her close, rubbing his hands up and down her back.

"Either way it's me. I'm trying to make up for everything that I took from you. We both know I never can. That night we were together I was your first. It should have been romantic and special. Not a frat party and then sex in your dorm room. And I knew it. Even then. I wanted to give you more, but I never had the chance. This is me making up for it. I know it's not enough. It will never be enough, but maybe this could be a start."

His words warmed her from the inside out. That cold dark place where the young woman she'd been cowered inside her was suddenly not so cold and definitely not dark. These were words she'd always longed to hear.

Words she'd never really thought she would hear. Kingsley had wounded her deeply—not the night he'd taken her virginity, but the next day when he'd cruelly turned her away.

And she had to remember it.

"That doesn't help, does it?" he asked. He dropped his arms and moved away from her.

She had a choice to make. She could keep punishing him for the past—and she could come up with a million reasons to justify that. Or—and it was a big thing—she could forgive him and accept this.

She took a deep breath. Fear held her where she was. Fear held her tongue. Fear had her wrapped in an icy grasp. She could let it go.

She needed to let it go.

"It does," she said at last.

She heard him exhale and he turned back to her.

"Good. Now let's drink these margaritas and you can tell me about your favorite things," he said.

"My favorite things?" she asked, picking up her glass and going to sit down on the padded bench again. "Like what? You already know I love Rob Thomas," she said with a wink.

"Still?" he asked, sitting down next to her.

"Yes."

"What other music do you like?"

"Taylor Swift, Ed Sheeran and Kanye."

"Love Kanye. Got to meet him in a club in Manhattan about a year ago," Kingsley said.

They kept talking about music and he found that he wasn't listening to what she said so much as he was enjoying the lyrical sound of her voice. When she was happy it was easy to hear it. And when she laughed everything inside him came alive.

Mrs. Tillman served dinner and then disappeared back inside the house. They ate and talked about politics, books and movies. He found that subjects that had never seemed too important to him when he talked with other people now seemed very vital with her. She made him feel alive and passionate about things he'd never given much weight to before.

"My cousins in Madrid have a lot to say about politics, and every time I visit the dinner conversation is always dominated by the climate in Europe."

He knew she was related through marriage to the Spanish royal family. Her cousin was married to the infanta. "Do you go to Spain a lot?"

"At least twice a year. Mom loves to visit her sister. You know, that's where I went when everything happened with you."

"I didn't know that. I was a little preoccupied with…"

"Getting yourself out of jail," she said. "Tell me about that."

"That's the last thing I want to talk about tonight," he said.

She took his hand in hers. She knew she had little choice but to deal with this. She wanted to understand the man he'd been back then because it went a long way toward explaining the man Kingsley was today.

"I just want to know a little more about what happened," she said. "You have questions about that night—I know you've been talking to our classmates—but I want to know about what happened after."

Kingsley pulled his hand from hers. "I know you do, but that time just stirs up anger and fear. I will be happy to discuss it with you another time. Just know that entire summer I was wishing that I could be with you."

Kingsley didn't want to talk about that night. Not now. He spent all of his free time trying to figure out how to fix what had happened, but tonight he wanted to be a regular guy. The kind of man who could romance a woman he was interested in.

But that wasn't who he was.

Was he fooling himself that they could ever be more than this—two people with a white-hot attraction between them and too much history?

He didn't think of himself as an idiot. So why was he always taking missteps with Gabi? He saw hesitation in her now. She had wrapped one arm around her own waist and he felt it. Those damned chains of the past. He was never going to be free of what had happened.

Even being set free and having those charges

dropped hadn't removed the stain. Were he and Hunter fooling themselves that finding the person responsible for Stacia's death was going to bring closure?

Until now, he hadn't thought so. He wasn't a defeatist so he refused to believe that this couldn't be fixed.

But tonight...tonight he'd been in a different head space. Now he was back to the world where doubt, vengeance and anger seemed to rule.

"I'm sorry. I didn't mean to bring that up," she said. "Why don't we go for a walk on the beach and pretend we are just like any other couple."

"Because we aren't," he said.

"No, we're not. But for tonight I was forgetting it," she said.

He could tell that she was sort of lying about it. But he let her get away with it because he wanted to pretend, too. Mrs. Tillman was in the house watching over Conner for this one night, so he knew it was safe for the both of them to be gone. He took her hand in his and she squeezed it tight.

For a minute he wished he were someone else. Anyone else. Just a regular guy with a normal job. Someone who maybe couldn't afford a nanny but needed a sweet, sexy woman like Gabi in his life.

Then the line blurred.

He was that lonely single dad. He had been for a while. Peri had made it easy for him to ignore the fact that his life had turned into all dad, all the time. Work was time-consuming, but most of the time he had staff to deal with the most demanding clients. He had the right people in place to help him with Conner. The only place where he was missing the right person was romantically.

Tonight he had been on the path to fixing that before the past had once again smacked him square in the jaw. And he was smarting from it.

He wanted to react the way he always did. Maybe carry Gabi into the house to his bedroom. Make love to her until he couldn't think anymore and then…then walk away. Get the hell out of California and give up on finding any closure. He would buy an island somewhere and homeschool Conner…except he wasn't a coward. He had never run from anything. He wasn't going to start now.

He led the way to the path down to the beach. "Why did you agree to this date? Did you feel like I owed you one?"

She watched her steps and when they got to a flat stretch of sand she stopped and turned to look at him. "No. I felt like I owed myself something. Everything that happened between us made me afraid to date guys I really liked. Made me think maybe I'd end up alone again. I never understood that I was trapped in that. I'm not saying I know what the future holds for us. But I'm not going to keep pretending that I don't want to be with you."

Her words humbled him. He'd told her his sin. Told her the truth that he'd been hiding from the world—and hell, from himself—for too long. But tonight none of that seemed to matter.

The sound of the waves on the shore lulled them as they walked slowly down the beach. She didn't speak and neither did he. He didn't want to. He just let the night close around them.

The breeze brought the scent of her perfume

and sometimes stirred the long strands of her hair so that they seemed to dance around her head.

"If you could have one thing, what would it be?" he asked.

He wanted to build a bridge between the past mistakes and the future he was beginning to realize he needed with her.

"I don't know. I've never thought about it. I'm always busy looking at my next business goal or planning a family get-together with my mom. What about you?"

"I want the past cleared up," he said. His focus on that account had never changed. Gabi had a life. She might think she had been hiding from relationships—and maybe she had been—but the rest of her life had gone on. And why shouldn't it? She'd been a bystander in the Stacia matter. Not a real participant.

"I bet. As I said, I'd be happy to help you contact those women on the list," she said.

"I…"

"Let me do this. I want more dates like this,

King, and we both know that until you get some closure you're not going to move forward."

He hadn't had anyone on his side with this except Hunter. Even Jade hadn't wanted to know about it. She'd liked that other people thought he was dangerous. "Okay. But if I see any backlash toward you or your business, you stop."

"Agreed," Gabi said. She stopped walking and looked out at the sea. He stood there next to her.

She turned toward him, wrapping her arms around his shoulders as she went up on tiptoe and kissed him. It was a sensual kiss. The one he'd been craving all night.

Deepening the kiss, he put his hands on the small of her back and lifted her off her feet so that she was pressed along the front of his body. The night breeze stirred around them, wrapping her hair around his neck and shoulders.

He was surrounded by her. He wanted to be naked. To feel her pressed all over him and to be inside her.

He needed that. He lifted his head and switched his hold on her, carrying her back up the path to the house. She just kept her arms wrapped around him, her fingers toying with the hair at the back of his neck until he entered his bedroom and closed the door behind him.

He let her slide down his body until her feet touched the ground. Then he kissed her, taking his time because he knew he wasn't leaving her again.

Ten

Gabi had often thought about that one night with Kingsley. But she didn't want to tonight. She wanted tonight to be new and about the people they were today, not about the past.

She sighed.

"What is it?"

"I...I just want this to be good, you know?"

He cupped her face in his hands and tilted her head back so he could stare down into her eyes. There was something elusive in his gaze. Something she wanted to identify but couldn't.

"It will be better than good," he said, lowering his mouth to hers.

His kiss swept aside the doubts she had about the past. The fire that had slowly been building between them since he'd first walked into her office now blazed out of control.

He caressed his way down from her neck, his fingers tracing a pattern over her skin that made her feel alive in a way she hadn't before. She sucked his lower lip into her mouth and pushed his jacket off his shoulders. His hands left hers as he shrugged out of it and he broke the kiss. His lips were wet and swollen from her kisses.

She watched him as he sauntered over to the closet to hang up his jacket. The light from the closet spilled out onto the floor and he turned to face her.

"I didn't take my time with you when we made love the first time. I want to tonight. But you get to me," he said.

"You get to me, too. I promised myself this time—"

"You'd be smarter?"

Yes. But she didn't want to admit that to him. "I was pretty smart the first time. I got exactly what I wanted that night."

"Did you?" he asked as he toed off his shoes and pulled off his tie.

She nodded. He'd undone the top button of his shirt and his feet were clad only in socks. This was such an intimate thing, she thought, watching a man disrobe. Most of the time when she had sex, they were hurried couplings in the dark. No time to consider if she was making a mistake or not.

But tonight this felt right.

"I did. What about you?"

"I feel the same way I did back then—like a boy about to get lucky for the first time."

"It wasn't your first time," she said quietly, walking over to him and pushing his hands aside. She undid the buttons of his dress shirt, the backs of her fingers brushing against the warm skin of his chest.

He tipped her chin up and looked down into her eyes. "But it was for you."

She nodded.

She'd never tried to hide the fact that she'd waited until she was in college to have sex. And if she were totally honest, she would have waited longer if Kingsley hadn't come along.

He made her crave things she'd never really wanted before. That was why she'd thought she loved him. Why she'd thought…what they had was special. She shook her head, trying to dispel those thoughts.

His shrewd gaze seemed to see all the way to her core. To the doubts that were gaining traction in her mind.

"Don't. I screwed up afterward, but we were good together. And we will be tonight," he said.

Then he cursed and dropped his hands and stepped back from her.

"Unless you've changed your mind," he said. "I won't pressure you."

She hadn't changed her mind. She just wanted to keep it clear in her head that he didn't love her. The fact that he was clearly aroused—she could see his erection pressing against the front of his trousers—but would still walk away if she wanted him to told a lot about the man he was.

And that man was one she wanted in her bed.

"I haven't changed my mind. I just don't want to go all emotional on you."

"How about lusty?" he asked.

She laughed. "Sure."

"Good. Lusty I can handle. Tonight let's just be young and in lust. I haven't had that in a really long time."

She hadn't, either. Being this close to Kingsley reminded her of the woman she'd once been. She needed to find her again tonight.

"Okay, lusty, let's do this."

Now he laughed. And then he smiled over at her, the expression on his face so sweet and almost vulnerable. "You are the only person I know who makes me feel...well, normal."

Normal.

For tonight that was enough.

She closed the gap between them and reached for his buttons again.

He put his hands on her hips and slowly drew her closer. She barely got his buttons undone before his mouth was on hers, kissing her with carnal intent. She felt his hands at the small of her back, drawing up her dress until the cool night air brushed over her buttocks and thighs.

She pushed her hands under the fabric of his shirt and wrapped them around his back just as he cupped her butt and drew her more firmly against the cradle of his hips.

His erection nudged at her and he shifted his stance so that he was rubbing against her center. She caught her breath and her nails dug into his back as he thrust his tongue deep into her mouth while moving his hips in the same rhythm.

They were both still fully clothed but it was one of the hottest things she'd ever experienced.

She sucked on his tongue as he pulled her panties down and she felt his big, warm hands on her bare flesh. He squeezed her buttocks and everything inside her clenched. She wriggled her legs until her panties fell to the floor. He lifted her up with his arm around her waist and took a step backward until he was leaning against the wall.

He held her against him as their mouths and bodies moved together.

He tasted so good, felt so good pressed against her. She wanted to slow down, to savor this moment, but it felt as if someone else had taken over her body. A woman she hardly recognized as herself, but at the same time, it felt so damned right.

She reached between their bodies, scraping her fingernail around his belly button. He tore his mouth from hers, breathing heavily as he looked down at her. No man had ever looked at her with so much desire in his eyes.

If she wasn't already close to the edge of her orgasm, that look would have driven her there. He tangled his hands in her hair and turned so that she was pressed between his body and the wall. He captured one of her hands in his, drew it up over her head and held it shackled to the wall while his mouth came back to hers.

He plundered her mouth. Made her forget everything, even where she ended and he began. She was a creature of fire in his arms and he was something that fed her flame. Drove her higher.

She gasped as she felt his fingers against her most intimate flesh. He drew a teasing pattern over her and then slowly parted her and tapped his finger on her clitoris. She shivered and shook in his arms, struggled to breathe as sensation started to wash over her.

She tried to pull back but there was nowhere to move. He kept tapping on her until her legs were moving frantically against him. Parting to give him greater access to her feminine secrets. His touch on her changed; he cupped her intimately between her legs as his thumb now rubbed over that sweet spot.

She felt his finger tracing the entrance of her body and then slowly he pushed it up inside her. She tore her mouth from his, moaning his name.

He kept pushing his finger higher inside her, going as deep as he could, while his thumb rocked against her. Everything inside her clenched and stars danced behind her closed eyes as she came.

It was harder and stronger than she'd climaxed before. She turned her head and found his shoulder, biting him through the fabric of his shirt while wave after wave of pleasure washed over her. He kept caressing her until she stopped shaking in his arms, and then he lifted her up and carried her over to the bed. He set her down on the edge and she collapsed backward, staring up at his ceiling, which had Spanish mission-style exposed beams and a big ceiling fan that spun lazily above her head.

She was numb with pleasure, shock waves still rocketing through her body.

Kingsley pushed himself to his feet and stepped away from Gabi. He wanted her so badly he felt as if he was going to lose all control. He turned away and took a deep breath. The first time they'd had sex he'd been a college guy with lust on his mind. This time he was a man and he wanted to take his time.

She shifted on the bed, leaning up on her elbows. Her clothing was disheveled and he wanted her naked. He slowly pushed his shirt off and let it fall to the floor.

She sat up and reached toward him. He felt the coolness of her long fingers against his skin. She moved them up his body at a leisurely pace as she got to her feet. She traced the tattoo of Conner's name that was over his heart.

His muscles flexed under her touch. As she

scraped her fingernail over the lettering, he felt goose bumps spread all over him. He wanted her. He was so damned close to losing all control.

She put her hands around his biceps. "I never told you, but one of the things that always attracted me to you was your arms."

"My arms?" he asked, struggling to make his voice sound normal and not guttural with need.

"Yes. I love how strong you are. Do you remember the day we met?"

"How could I forget it?" He'd stumbled into her after leaving the gym and almost flattened her. He'd grabbed her and rolled so that he was under her when they fell. And he'd been a goner. He'd had to get to know the woman who had turned him on with one brush of her body against his.

He lowered his mouth to hers, unable to wait another second. He didn't want to discuss the past. He wanted to get her naked and bury himself inside her. Get so deep that nothing would matter except the two of them.

She rose on her tiptoes and tightened her grip on his upper arms. He lifted her again, wrapping his arms around her hips before breaking the kiss and letting her slide slowly down his body.

She reached between them for his belt and while she worked at freeing him from his pants, he found the zipper to her dress and pushed it off her body.

He stepped back as the fabric fell away from her to pool around her feet. She wore only her high heels and a flesh-colored bra. She reached behind her and undid the fastening of her bra, shrugged her shoulders and let it fall to the floor.

She shook her head and her hair danced around her shoulders as she crooked her finger at him. "Come closer."

He shoved his pants and underwear down his legs and kicked them off. He caught her with one arm around her waist and maneuvered them down to the bed, carefully keeping his weight on his free arm. She parted her legs and he settled between them. Her hands skimmed up and down his back as he pulled his hips back, reveling in the naked feel of her flesh against his.

Naked.

Damn.

"Are you on the pill?" he asked.

"Yes," she said.

"Good."

"Good?"

"Yes. I want to feel all of you, Gabi. Against all of me."

"Me, too," she said.

He lifted himself up on his elbows so he could look down into her brown eyes. He framed her face with his hands and stroked his thumbs over her cheekbones before slowly moving them lower. He followed the path of his hands with his mouth. Kissing her face and then moving down the side of her neck. He traced her collarbone and found a small scar right above her left breast.

He cupped both of her breasts and stroked his finger over one nipple while he sucked the other one into his mouth. He let his hands move lower over her ribs to her waist. He lifted his mouth from her breast and dropped kisses around her belly button, watching as she shifted against him, her legs moving restlessly.

He continued moving lower, placing his palm

over her mound and rubbing before shifting his touch to her most intimate flesh. He traced the opening of her body, and her hips jerked upward against him. She opened her legs wider and he pulled his hand from her and replaced it with his erection.

He drew back his hips and slowly entered her. Grabbed her hands with his and stretched them up over her head as he fully seated himself inside her.

Their eyes met.

He felt that contact all the way to his soul as he started thrusting into her. He went slowly at first, feeling the way her body tightened around him each time. Hearing her gasps and how her breath quickened. He wanted the moment to last but felt his climax closing in on him.

He wanted them to orgasm together and pulled one hand free to reach between their bodies and flick his finger over her clit.

She cried his name and he felt her tightening around him as she arched her back and rocked her hips frantically against his. He buried his head in her neck and thrust harder and deeper than before, driving himself toward climax.

When they had both climaxed, she wrapped her arms and legs around him and stroked her hands up and down his back. She kissed his shoulder and rested her cheek against it.

He lowered his head to her chest, heard the hammering of her heart underneath him. He was careful to keep her from feeling all of his weight.

When he could breathe again, he got up and cleaned them both up. Then he tucked her into his bed and climbed in next to her.

"What are you doing?"

"What I should have done the first time," he said. "Staying with you all night."

She didn't say anything, just curled against him and fell asleep. He stayed awake, though. Knowing that his life would have been very different if he'd done this the last time.

Eleven

The county commissioners were mostly nice people who wanted to make the county better for the citizens who lived here. Her mom had served back in the early nineties and they'd done lots of good projects, like this playground that had been cutting-edge in the 1990s but was now out-of-date and sadly in need of repair.

But all of that was going to be taken care of today. She had the check from Kingsley in her pocket. The plans from the playground engineer she'd hired were in her bag. She had the feeling that she could do anything.

Sure, she was willing to admit the possibility that fantastic sex with Kingsley was partially responsible for her mood. But the truth was that she knew it was more than sex. When she'd woken in his arms this morning and looked over at his face and saw him watching her…she felt something electric pass between them.

Something.

Well, it felt like a hell of a lot more than lust. Was it love?

Love.

It scared her to think how all-encompassing the feeling was. She had to fight the urge to text Kingsley. Just to see how he was doing. Because she missed him.

She'd left his mansion at 7:00 a.m. and had been away from him for a mere three hours. But already she missed him.

Just a month ago she would have been happy to never see him darken her door again but now he made the day seem sunnier.

Damn.

This would be funny if it were happening to someone else. But it was her. And she knew that she wouldn't have it any other way.

She daydreamed about her life with Kingsley and Conner. Thought of them as a picture-perfect little family.

She wasn't really ready to be a mom. And things were complicated with Kingsley. No matter how many dreams she spun in her head, the reality was he was fixated on the past. A past that she was finally finding closure to.

She toyed with the sunburst charm on her necklace as it hit her that she might not have a happy ending with Kingsley. That these emotions that felt like love to her might just be a vehicle for her to move on.

She didn't like the way that thought made her feel.

"Ms. de la Cruz, please follow me. The commissioners are ready for you now."

Gabi followed the young assistant down the hall to the boardroom. She'd been in this room many times before. First as a young girl meeting her mom and then as an adult arguing for more funding for projects for kids and discussing the preliminary planning for the playground. She felt a little nervous as she smoothed her hands down the back of her linen skirt and then ex-haled all those nerves out the way she'd learned from her mom all those years ago.

She had this.

Money had been the only stumbling block, and right now she had a check worth more than the commissioners thought the park and recreation center would cost.

"Good afternoon, everyone," she said as she entered the room.

There was a round of greetings and she took a seat after passing out her presentation books. She knew it was the digital age, but she liked paper. She made her presentation feeling the confidence of knowing that there was no way they could turn her down this time.

"Thank you, Gabi. The design you have come up with meets all of our criteria for incorporat-ing the local landscape while at the same time making it a fun and exciting area for the com-munity," Commissioner Ortiz said.

"I like that you've made the focus on children but also included facilities for adults, as well," Mrs. O'Malley said.

Gabi smiled at them. "And I've secured funding. So the only thing we are waiting on to take this project from dream to reality is your approval."

"Well…" Mr. Ortiz said.

"Well? Do you all have an objection?" Gabi asked. She couldn't think of a single thing that was standing in their way.

"We didn't realize that you'd secured funding from Kingsley Buchanan."

"He's a former college sports star and well-known. Why is that a problem?" Gabi asked.

Mrs. O'Malley looked at the other members of the board. All of whom refused to meet her gaze. Gabi felt an icy lump form in the pit of her stomach. Kingsley was their problem?

Finally Mrs. O'Malley leaned forward, leveling her steady gaze on Gabi.

"He's just not the sort of person that this town wants to name things after," she said at last.

"Football star? Single dad? Wealthy businessman? I don't understand your objection, especially since he doesn't expect you to name the facility after him," Gabi said. It was no longer about her playground, though she was still determined to see it go through. No, this was about Kingsley. Were these people honestly not going to accept his money because of charges against him that had been dropped more than ten years ago?

"It's about his arrest," Mr. Ortiz said.

"The charges were dropped," Gabi said. "He has been a free man for more than ten years."

"But many questions remain," Mr. Ortiz said. "And some in our community… Well, we just want the park to be unencumbered by any gossip."

She was angry but she kept her cool. Was this what Kingsley had to deal with? She had an inkling of why resolving the past was so important to him.

Mrs. O'Malley leaned forward. "I don't like it any more than you do, but the cold, hard facts are that several families that live in our city were affected by the frat-house murder and I think things would be better if his name wasn't involved."

"Very well. Thank you for your time," Gabi said, gathering her presentation booklets and walking out the door.

* * *

Kingsley didn't like the fact that he'd lied to Gabi, but telling her he was going to their old university to dig through witness statements made to campus security—well, he didn't think she'd approve. She had agreed to contact the women from Daria Miller's files, but he didn't want her involved any further than that.

A part of him wished he could drop it, but he couldn't.

It would be easier for Gabi if he did. She wasn't really involved in the incident. For her there were more traumas around the fact that he'd had sex with her and then left her.

He got that.

He knew that he had a lot to make up for on that front and he was willing to do whatever he had to in order to make that happen.

It surprised him how much she meant to him. He wasn't saying it was love—lust was about where he felt comfortable—but he wanted her to stay with him. He was looking forward to getting home and spending the evening with her and Conner, and then after Conner was in bed spending time alone with her.

Damn.

He had it bad and he knew it.

He pulled the huge archival box of witness statements closer to him. Better to focus on fixing the past. He liked the thought that he'd figure out what happened and fix it, enabling both Hunter and him to move on. Fixing things had long been something that mattered to him.

When he opened the box he was surprised to see how many statements were in there. He pulled a stack out and glanced into the box to see Gabi's name on one.

He hadn't known she'd made a statement. The DA hadn't mentioned her at all.

Maybe she hadn't mentioned him. So they wouldn't have known she and he had been together the night Stacia was killed.

He pulled her statement out and read it.

Well, this made no sense. Not only had she talked about him, she'd also said he spent the night at her place and she'd woken up to find him gone. Which wasn't what had happened.

He couldn't think of a single reason why she would lie unless she was covering for him.

He realized right then how badly it must have hurt her when he rejected her at the jailhouse. She'd come there ready to support him and help him out of a tight spot. And he'd gone into full protective mode, not wanting anything to happen to her. Not wanting her to be colored with the same brush that he and Hunter were.

He'd known that things were going to get ugly. Even his attorney—his own brother, Ben—had thought he was guilty and talked to him about cutting a plea deal. Gabi might be one of only two people to believe he hadn't been involved in Stacia's killing. Hunter being the other one.

Wow.

This changed things.

It made him see her in a different light. He'd always known the attraction between them was powerful, but this went deeper. This was a kind of attachment he hadn't let himself believe existed.

She had to have thought she was in love with him.

Kingsley divided the statements into two piles

and was amazed at how big the file of statements he hadn't known about was. He skimmed all the ones he'd already read a dozen times. The ones that the DA had presented in order to have Hunter and him arrested. No wonder Ben had said to leave this alone. As he flipped through the documents he saw statements from people he'd thought were his friends. They'd told how he was always with another girl—not entirely untrue—and that he seemed to date each one for less than a month.

Gabi fit that profile, he realized. But he'd been planning to stay with her. Not that any of that mattered now.

He started reading through the statements that were new to him, and Hunter arrived when he was a third of the way into that stack.

"Did you know that Chuck gave a statement that night?" Kingsley asked once Hunter was up to speed on what he'd found.

"No. What did he say?"

"That we never left the common room after Stacia left. And we were in a corner drinking and laughing."

"Not sure that helps us, but at least he saw us there," Hunter said. Hunter pulled out his tablet and stylus and started making notes on it. "Have you sorted them at all?"

"Yes. These are the ones who all corroborate the DA's version of events, the ones we read at the archives. These are the ones that are different versions."

"Anything helpful like Chuck's?"

"Some. Some of them just mention that we were both at the parties where other girls had been given the date-rape drug. And Cassidy Freeman said you told her that you liked having sex with women who were passed out."

"Bitch."

"That's not helpful," Kingsley said. "Did you really say that?"

Hunter gave him a hard glare. "No. She was always after me but you know I was into Stacia in those days. And I used to be a one-woman man."

Kingsley reached over and squeezed his friend's shoulder. So much had changed. These statements about himself and Hunter were about men he no longer recognized. They weren't the life of the party anymore... And he couldn't remember the last time he and Hunter had laughed together unless it was over something silly Conner did.

"Let's make a list of everyone who placed us at the frat house and those who thought we did it. Then we can contact them and see what they remember," Hunter said.

"What makes you think they will talk to us now?" Kingsley asked. He wasn't sure that they were going to get answers from people who thought they did it.

"I don't know. I thought... I had hoped this would be easier. That we'd find something that pointed the finger at someone else."

"Me, too, buddy," he said. "Let's just get this stuff sorted and then we can ask Daria to contact some of the people who think we are guilty."

"Good idea," Kingsley said. They both worked for the next two hours and when they were done, Kingsley had an idea why all of these statements hadn't been used. A lot of them were conflicting. He'd read two statements from people he remembered not being at the party. "Joe Falcone was in Detroit that night. I'm not sure I trust his statement."

"I know. This wasn't helpful at all. It clarified nothing," Hunter said. "We're no closer to finding out what really happened than we were yesterday."

Kingsley agreed. But he wasn't giving up. "Let's see if there is anything else that these statements have in common. I remember reading that Stacia left the party and came back. But I have to be honest, I'm a little foggy on when that was. I think I remember seeing her again. What about you?"

Hunter shrugged. "I can only recall the part of the night before you and I sat down and started doing shots."

Kingsley had the feeling that Hunter was hiding something. It was the way he looked past him instead of meeting his eyes. But just then, Kingsley's phone rang and he saw that it was Gabi.

"I have to take this."

Hunter nodded and Kingsley went outside

to talk to Gabi. He needed something that was fresh and clean, not the murkiness of the past.

Gabi left the meeting with her hands shaking and got in her car. Instead of driving back to the office, she headed out to the Pacific Coast Highway. Without regard for speed, she drove the roads she knew like the back of her hand as if she was running for her life.

And she guessed she was. All those nice, safe thoughts that she had about maybe loving Kingsley and finding closure were gone. She realized that until he found Stacia's killer, the stigma of the past was always going to hang over him and by extension anyone who was associated with him.

It made her mad and shattered her illusions about the justice system. She'd always believed what the court said. She hadn't questioned their judgments because her father was a judge and she knew he was a good and righteous man. But today she realized that some people got their facts from the court of public opinion.

She pulled over and rested her head on the steering wheel. What was she going to do?

She picked up her phone and dialed her father's number without a second thought.

"Gabi, how are you?"

"I'm good, Papi," she said.

"What can I do for you? Your mother said you are bringing a man to brunch," he said.

"I am. He's the guy I dated in college. He's a single dad now and we are bringing his three-year-old son."

"Interesting," he said.

"What does that mean?"

"Simply that I always thought you had unfinished business with him."

"I do."

"You okay, princess?"

She smiled to herself. Her father was the one man she knew would have her back even if she was wrong. She realized she'd called him because she needed to dispel the anger and disappointment she'd felt after leaving the meeting.

"Yes, Papi, I am."

"Good. I have to go, but look forward to seeing you Sunday."

"Me, too. Love you."

"Love you, too, princess."

She turned the car around and drove back to her office, where she found Conner playing with a pair of twins about his age. He ran over and gave her a hug when he saw her. She looked over at Abby, who was watching the kids.

"Where's Melissa?"

"In a meeting with the parents," Abby said. "They are looking for a nanny."

"When Melissa gets out, would you ask her to come and see me? Conner, are you okay? Do you want to come and help me work?" Gabi asked.

Conner looked up at her, his face so like Kingsley's. "I want to keep playing with my friends."

"Sounds good. My office is right down the hall. If you need me, come and get me."

He nodded and ran back over to the twins to keep playing.

She entered her office and drafted an email to send to the county commissioners. And then printed it out for Melissa to review. She was still angry and didn't want to say anything she'd regret. She needed an unbiased opinion.

She worked on her column until Melissa came down to join her. "Great news. I think I got my first clients."

"Congratulations. When do they want us to start? Mae is coming back on Monday."

"I know. I mentioned that to them and scheduled an in-home visit for then."

"Good job," Gabi said. Melissa didn't need her to micromanage things.

"Thanks. The twins and Conner are really getting along well and the parents—Daisy and Scott Banner—wanted to set up a playdate with him."

"I'll go and talk to them. And then I'll have to call Kingsley. I'm not sure how he feels about having other kids to his place."

Melissa led the way back to the playroom and Gabi talked to the parents of the twins. They were very friendly and clearly doted on their little boys. Daisy was a food blogger who had recently been approached by the Food Network to star in her own show and Scott was a champion deep-sea fisherman. Apparently that was a thing.

"I'm glad you're considering using our agency for your sons. I understand you'd like a playdate with Conner," Gabi said after introductions were made.

"Please, Gammi, I really like Ty and Doug," Conner said, coming over to her.

She ruffled his hair. "I think it's a great idea. I have to check with your dad and then we can figure out the logistics. You keep playing while we do that," Gabi said.

Conner nodded and the boys went back to their playing. She overheard him telling them about how knights were fighters but did it for honor. One of the boys asked what honor was and Conner shrugged and said, "Something good." She smiled.

"Conner lives outside Carmel. His father is very protective of Conner, so I think the playdate would have to be at his place. Are you okay with that?" she asked.

Daisy looked at Scott and he nodded.

"Okay. Let me call Kingsley and I'll be right back."

Gabi went down the hall to her office and dialed Kingsley's number.

"Hey, you," he said by way of greeting.

"Hey. How's your meeting?" she asked. He'd told her he was going to meet with a prospective new client for his sports agency. It wasn't surprising to her that their old alma mater had another Heisman Trophy winner. Their school was known for excellence in all sports.

"Long and a little bit boring," he said. "What's up?"

"Conner has made friends with some twins and wants to have a playdate."

"How did he meet other kids?" Kingsley asked.

She explained the situation.

"I'm not sure I'm ready for my little man to be at someone else's house with parents I don't even know."

"I figured that. So I suggested they come to your place," she said.

"I don't want to advertise where we live, but Conner hasn't really played with his kids his

age before." Kingsley hesitated. "Okay. I guess
it would be fine if he had them over."

"Good. I will make the arrangements. Will
you be home for dinner?" she asked.

"I will. It's been a long day," he said.

"For me, too. I'll be happy to be back at our
home."

As soon as she said it, she realized that it was
Kingsley's home and not hers.

"I'll be glad to be at our home too."

He disconnected the call and she had to tell
herself that it was nothing. He hadn't just re-
ferred to his house as their home. But in her
heart she knew he had.

Twelve

Kingsley got home to find a big bedouin-style tent set up in the backyard. He assumed it was Conner's big playdate, which made him a little nervous. His son had never really played with other kids and he wanted it to be perfect.

Gabi had certainly pulled out all the stops with the tent. He walked into the kitchen and found Mrs. Tillman playing her online bingo game.

"Hello, sir. Do you need anything from me?" Mrs. Tillman asked.

"Not at all. Are the other kids still here?" he asked. "What are our dinner plans?"

"There aren't any other kids here. Gabi has

dinner covered and asked me to send you out back when you got home. She said you're camping out."

"What happened to Conner's playdate?" he asked Mrs. Tillman.

She shrugged. "I don't know the details, but Gabi did say that her agency wouldn't be taking the parents on as clients."

He didn't like the sound of that. He took his phone out of his pocket as he went into his room to get changed. There were no messages from Gabi so he would have to get the scoop from her once he was out in the backyard.

He changed into a pair of faded jeans and his old team jersey before heading out back. As he got closer to the tent he noticed that the fire pit had been moved from the patio and now sat in front of the tent area. There was a clay tagine suspended over the fire that emitted some delicious smells.

He pulled back the flap to the tent and poked his head inside.

Gabi and Conner were sitting on a mound of

sumptuous-looking pillows in a scene that was straight out of *The Arabian Nights.*

"Daddy!"

Conner scrambled to his feet and ran over to him. He scooped his son up and kissed the top of his head before setting him back down.

"I told Conner he couldn't have his playdate tonight because you wanted to surprise him with this campout," Gabi said.

Kingsley looked at her and saw fire in her eyes. He was beginning to suspect that the other parents wouldn't let their kids play with his son once they'd learned who he was.

"I did. I hope you don't mind."

"Not at all. We've been reading about knights. But these are different than the ones I learned about before," Conner said.

Conner took Kingsley's hand and led him over to where Gabi was seated. When they were both settled onto the pillows, Kingsley noticed an old-fashioned illuminated book on Gabi's lap. There were illustrations of knights with curved swords.

Conner climbed onto Kingsley's lap and Gabi

went back to finishing the story they were reading, which was the tale of Aladdin.

"That was so exciting. I wish we had a secret cave," Conner said when she was finished.

"Me, too," Kingsley said.

"For tonight we do. In the trunk over there is everything you will need to go on an adventure like Aladdin. Go and check it out, Conner," Gabi said.

His son jumped up and ran to the other side of the tent. He opened the trunk and exclaimed excitedly as he started pulling out costumes, toy swords and a map.

"Why did you do all of this?" Kingsley asked.

"Because Conner deserved it," Gabi said.

"What about the playdate?" Kingsley asked.

"It didn't work out. The timing was wrong," she said, getting to her feet and walking over to Conner.

"What's this?" Conner held up a gossamer-thin piece of fabric.

"That's for my costume. I'm going to be one of those dashing ladies we read about. You and your dad are Aladdin and his band of thieves.

Put on your costumes and meet me by the steps leading to the beach," she said. She took the pieces that made up her costume.

And Kingsley pushed aside his worries for the night and went to help his son get into costume. Conner talked excitedly the entire time. Once they were both dressed they went outside to find Gabi in her harem-girl outfit wearing a veil over her face.

Kingsley's breath caught in his chest as he looked at her. And he was struck with the realization that he wanted her in his life. Forever.

He wasn't sure he could have her. He'd never really had a chance to figure out how to make things work in a relationship, and he suspected it might be due to the fact that he'd screwed up with her.

"You're gorgeous."

"So are you," she said. "Both of you. Conner, let me take your picture with your daddy."

"With our swords out," Conner insisted. They both drew their swords and posed next to each other as Gabi took a few pictures with her phone.

"Now all three of us," Conner said.

Gabi came over to them and Kingsley wrapped his arm around Gabi as she lifted Conner up between them. Kingsley extended his arm and got them all in the frame before snapping the selfie.

"Let's look at it," Gabi said. They stared down at the picture of the three of them.

"It's like we are a family," Conner said.

It was like that.

"But I'm just your nanny," Gabi reminded his son.

He could tell Conner didn't like that—and truth to tell he didn't, either—but tonight wasn't the time to get into it.

"Did you bring the map?" Gabi asked, changing the subject.

"I did," Conner said, pulling it out of his pocket.

They followed the map down the path to the beach and then got to a stone circle with a big X drawn in the sand.

"What now?" Kingsley asked.

"Now we dig," Conner said.

They all dug until they uncovered another chest, and when Kingsley removed it he wondered what they'd find inside. Conner opened it and exclaimed. It was full of toy gold coins and trinkets just such as the ones the book had described.

Conner was over the moon with his treasure and Kingsley realized that the day he'd blackmailed Gabi into being Conner's nanny had been the most fortuitous one of his life. He'd found a treasure he hadn't realized he'd been searching for.

Brunch with her parents made her more nervous than facing an entire room of spoiled children and being told she was the one adult that had to get them in line. On the way there, Conner seemed fine in the backseat of the SUV and Kingsley... It was hard to get a good read on him. He had on his Wayfarers.

Kidz Bop music filled the car. To be honest, that might be part of her nerves. She was also still on edge over the canceled playdate with the twins. Once their parents had heard Kingsley's name, they'd pulled out. It bothered her.

She'd been really upset but Conner had taken

it in stride when she'd told him that his friends would have to play another day due to the fact that his dad had planned a campout under the stars. She'd told a similar white lie to Kingsley so that he wouldn't have to know that the parents hadn't wanted their kids to play with Conner.

It all made her so mad.

They'd slept in the tent Gabi had brought over, a gift from a sheikh her cousin Gui knew. That summer she'd spent in Spain she'd met all sorts of interesting people. Even men who fancied themselves in love with her. But she had been too confused and scarred by what had happened to be any good to anyone.

"What's up?" Kingsley said.

"Nervous."

"Why?" he asked. "You like your parents, right?"

She laughed. She loved her parents. "Yes. My brother and I get along, as well. He has a new girlfriend. And it must be serious if he's bringing her home."

"Is it serious with us?" he asked. "Is that what's making you nervous?"

She leaned her head back against the leather seat, glad her large sunglasses concealed her eyes from him. She was serious about Kingsley. But she was seeing every day how much of a struggle it was going to be to live here where everyone knew his story and still be happy.

"Yes," she said. "Does that make you want to jump out on the side of the road and run for the hills?"

"Not at all. It makes me want to lock the doors so you can't get out," he said, reaching over to take her hand in his. He lifted it to his mouth and kissed the back of it, then put her hand on his thigh. "But if you're not nervous about brunch, that means you can only be nervous because you didn't tell me the truth."

"What?"

"I know about what really happened," he said. "I don't understand why you haven't said anything."

She glanced in the backseat and noticed that Conner had put his headphones on and switched on a movie.

"I didn't want to upset you. I was mad enough

for the both of us. And really, there was nothing to be done to change their minds, so I just kept it to myself. I do think we made the evening a lot of fun for Conner. And I told Melissa we won't be taking them on as clients at the firm."

"What are you talking about?" he asked. "I meant what went on at the county commissioners' meeting. I heard they don't want my money involved with the playground project."

"Oh, that," she said. "It was a rough day, Kingsley. First the commissioners and then the twins' parents. Until that moment I never realized what you lived with."

"It's not that bad on the East Coast or in big cities. But Carmel is too close to the campus."

"I was thinking the same thing. You should move back east," she said.

"Would you?"

"No. California is in my blood. It's my home. I couldn't live somewhere else and feel whole," she said. "Besides, I wouldn't want to let the jerks win."

He gave her a half smile.

"Me, neither. Which is why I'm here."

"You said revenge. And I honestly thought you should be more willing to let it go. That revenge never solves anything, but when I thought of how Conner would feel if he knew the truth... well, I get it."

She felt protective of Conner and not just because he was her temporary charge. She knew it was a mistake to get attached to Conner. There were no guarantees with herself and Kingsley, but she couldn't help it. Both of the Buchanan men had cast a spell on her.

She didn't want to break it.

"Tell me where you are in your investigation," she said.

Kingsley told her about all of the witness statements and how many there were that he'd never read before.

"I read yours," he said at last. "You lied."

She blushed and pulled her hand back. "I didn't. I just said that when I woke up you were gone."

"You and I both know that you were awake when I left your room," he pointed out.

"Yes. But...you know I fancied myself in love

with you, Kingsley. I wanted to protect you in any way I could. But then—"

"I was an ass. I should have said thank you. I should have been nicer when you visited me at the jailhouse."

"Yes, you should have," she said. "Why weren't you?"

"Hours were going by and I was beginning to realize that it wasn't just a misunderstanding and the cops were definitely going to charge us. I didn't remember killing anyone and thought we were being framed. I still do. And I didn't want you anywhere near that mess."

"It was the only place I wanted to be. But perhaps you were right. I didn't need to be there."

He followed the GPS directions and turned in to the development where her parents lived. They had a sprawling Mexican hacienda-style house with a big circular drive. Kingsley parked behind a classic '69 Corvette.

He got Conner out of his car seat and took his hand as they walked up to the front door. Conner reached up and took Gabi's, as well.

She was struck by how they were a unit now.

The past and future all disappeared and there was only the present and this little family she'd found. The family she'd always sort of wanted but never thought would be hers, which was why she'd frozen last night when Conner had called them that—a family.

Gabi's parents' house was elegant, sophisticated and very homey. But the fact that her father was a federal judge made Kingsley a little nervous. He shouldn't be, because his own brother was a lawyer and his father a CEO of a big conglomerate.

Maybe it came down to the fact that Javier was Gabi's father, not that he was a judge. Javier was the father who knew Kingsley had been arrested. The father who had seen his daughter upset and had to send her out of the country to recover.

Now Javier had invited Kingsley over to the grill for a beer and he suspected a serious conversation was coming.

"Your son is adorable," Javier said. "I remember when Alejandro was that age. They grow up fast."

The older man held a beer in one hand and a spatula in the other. The chicken had been dry rubbed with some sort of spice combination that smelled delicious. Not for the first time, Kingsley wished that he was just a regular guy enjoying a barbecue.

"Yes, they do. Seems like I was carrying him everywhere just yesterday," Kingsley said. He remembered the first time he held Conner in his arms. He knew then that he had to stop ignoring the past and fix it. Because he didn't want his son to deal with the repercussion of his actions.

"You want to protect him," Javier said.

It wasn't a question but a statement.

"Yes."

"That's the burden and blessing of fatherhood. My own father said this to me one time and I thought, *the old man thinks he's Cervantes*."

Kingsley smiled at that. "I get it. It makes no sense until you have your own kid, though."

"Exactly. I like you, Kingsley. I have seen you rise from the ashes of something that would have kept a lesser man down, but you just brushed yourself off and moved on. That takes *cojones*."

"Thanks." He wasn't sure where this was going. He heard the *but* in Javier's voice.

"Gabi is my princess. I know she's not perfect and that she has her flaws, but in my eyes she is faultless and I want her to have everything her heart desires."

"I want that, too, sir," Kingsley said.

"Good. If you hurt her, I'll visit the same pain back on you, and this time you will find it harder to rise from the ashes, understand?"

Kingsley nodded. "You should know I never would hurt her. I protected her the last time."

"I know. You sent her away. I wasn't sure if you did it because you didn't care for her or if you did it to protect her. I'm still not sure, but it was the best thing for her. It made her stronger."

"Papi, are you talking about me?" Gabi said, coming over and slipping her hand into Kingsley's.

"I'm warning him not to hurt you, princess," Javier said with a jovial grin.

Kingsley got the impression that Javier didn't hide anything from his family. Kingsley thought his parents would like Gabi's. The two families had a lot in common.

"Thanks, Papi, but I'm a big girl now. I can handle this."

Javier leaned over and kissed Gabi's forehead. "In case you can't, I've got your back."

She laughed but Javier leveled a very serious look at Kingsley. He wrapped his arm around Gabi and led her away from the grill and her father.

Conner was sitting on the big bench swing under the shade of a ponderosa pine tree in the corner of the yard. Kingsley led Gabi over there.

"I hope my dad wasn't too...too parental," she said.

"It's good. I can handle it. I'd be more worried if he wasn't protective of his kids," Kingsley said.

"He's definitely that," she said.

"Daddy," Conner said as they approached. "Will you push me on the swing?"

"Sure will, buddy. That's why I came over here," Kingsley said.

"Come on, Gammi," Conner said, patting the bench next to him.

Gabi sat by his son and Kingsley stood there for a minute feeling—overwhelmed. He wanted this family to be real. But right now he was distracted from the one thing that could bring him that dream.

He needed to focus on finding out who had killed Stacia or he was never going to have any closure. He was never going to be able to put the past to rest.

Anger like he hadn't felt since the night he'd been arrested welled up inside him. Whoever had killed Stacia and kept silent about it had stolen this from him. Had taken the life he might have had away from him.

He had been lucky to have Conner—God knew, that was the truth. But he could have had Gabi and maybe they could have had a few more kids. But now they couldn't—until the specter of the past was gone.

She wouldn't want to raise kids no one wanted to play with. Hell, neither did he.

"Kingsley?"

"Yes?"

"Conner asked if you wanted to sit with us. We can swing it together."

"Yes," he said. He sat down, more determined than ever to find the person who was blocking his second chance with Gabi and to make him pay.

Thirteen

Alejandro joined Gabi in the butler's pantry when she went to make more margaritas to go with brunch. His girlfriend, Eva, was funny, gorgeous and smart. She was a human rights lawyer who worked all over the world.

Gabi was proud of the business she'd built, but talking about kids and parenting issues after Eva had just finished telling them about the clean water campaign she'd spearheaded in Central America had made Gabi feel… Well, as though she should be sitting at the kids' table.

"What do you think of Eva?" Alejandro asked.

"Scary awesome," Gabi said. "I like her, but I

think if I had to be around her too often I'd start to hate myself."

"Really?" Alejandro asked. "She told me she's jealous that you have your own business."

"She did?" she asked.

"Yes. She's tired of traveling all the time. She's thinking of settling down…"

It was funny how perspective changed things. Gabi's life looked good to Eva because it was very normal and Eva's sounded exciting to Gabi because…well, if she were being honest, because it would take her away from all the uncertainty she felt around Kingsley.

"With you?" she asked her brother.

"Yes. We've been dating for a year now," Ali said.

"Why are you just now bringing her home?" Gabi asked.

Ali shrugged and reached around her to dump lime juice into the blender. "You see what she's like. I met her when I was at Gui's last summer and we hooked up, but we were both on vacation, you know."

She did know. "So when did you meet again?"

"I called her from the airport when I got home and told her I wanted to see her again. I couldn't stop thinking about her, Gabi. I didn't know if it was just obsession or real affection," Alejandro said.

"How did you figure it out?" she asked her brother. He was eighteen months older than her and they'd always been close. She wanted to know if he had any insights into love that might help her.

She knew that Ali's situation was different than hers. Eva didn't have a past like Kingsley, but love...love was the great equalizer. She'd read that somewhere and it had resonated with her.

"I'm not sure. We've been living together for the last few months. Both of us still travel a lot but I know she's there."

"Is it convenience?" Gabi asked. "I feel like that with Kingsley, because I'm living at his place to be a nanny to Conner. Like maybe just living there is making me see us as something we aren't."

She dumped the ice into the blender and added the tequila but didn't turn it on.

"I see the way he looks at you, Gabs. Whatever he feels for you is intense. I'd say it was love, but I don't know him well enough," Alejandro said. "I know Dad warned him not to hurt you, but I don't think that was necessary."

She agreed. Kingsley would never intentionally hurt her. But he would do whatever he thought was necessary to keep her safe. And if that meant going after revenge or cutting her from his life, she knew he would do it.

She turned on the blender and moments later Ali poured the frozen margaritas into the pitcher.

"I'm glad you have Eva. Maybe I can come over for dinner one night and get to know her without Mom being all nosy."

"Ha. You'll report back to Mom."

"Of course I will. But it would still be nice."

"Sounds like a plan," Alejandro said.

They rejoined everyone on the patio, where Conner was "reading" to her mom and dad from his iPad.

Watching her parents interact with Conner

made her realize that they probably wanted grandchildren. Yet they never pressured her or Ali to have kids. It was as if they knew that families couldn't be forced.

Of course they knew that.

"Margarita refills?" Gabi asked.

Kingsley turned and smiled at her and all the doubts that invaded her thoughts when they weren't together disappeared. Seeing him made her happy. Made her believe that whatever else was happening in the world couldn't affect them or hurt them.

"I'm driving, so no more for me," Kingsley said.

"I'm not, so, yes, please," Eva said.

"Me, too," Gabi's mom said.

After she refilled the glasses she sat back down next to Kingsley.

"You were gone awhile. Everything okay with your brother?"

"Yes. Just talking about how spectacular Eva is."

"I am, aren't I?" Eva said with a laugh.

"Yes, you are," Alejandro said.

"You're not so bad yourself," Eva said.

"To my brother!" Gabi said, lifting her glass.

Everyone lifted their glasses.

"What are you doing?" Conner asked.

"It's called toasting," Kingsley explained. "It's a way of saying good job to someone."

"To my daddy!" Conner said, lifting his sippy cup.

Everyone again lifted their glasses.

Conner then went around the table and toasted everyone who was there, including her parents' dachshunds, Gia and Marlow.

She glanced over at Kingsley as she heard him laugh. He had so much affection for his son. She thought again about the way the county commissioners hadn't wanted Kingsley's involvement with the playground and decided she was going to fight them. Because he was a good man. She saw that not only when he was with his son but with everyone.

He could have taken offense to her father's warning, but he hadn't.

Kingsley glanced over at her and she didn't look away. She saw the man he was with all his flaws and strengths. She wanted to accept him as he was.

"You're staring at me," he said.

"I like looking at you."

"I like it, too," he said. Lifting his hand, he twined their fingers together and she felt as though they were on the same page. They wanted the same things from life, and together they would make that happen.

O'Hannigans was a California institution. Nestled on one of the curves of the Pacific Coast Highway, it afforded great views of endless blue sky and sun-drenched ocean. Gabi parked her car in one of the spots around back and pushed her sunglasses up on top of her head as she got out and walked into the restaurant.

It had been two weeks since they'd had brunch at her parents' house and she and Kingsley had grown closer—sort of. They were as close as two people who had white-hot sex every night and went their separate ways during the day could be.

He'd had to go to the East Coast for a client

for three days, and when he was home, he and Hunter were locked in his office trying to piece together what had happened the night Stacia had died.

She hoped this meeting with her friends from college would reveal something—anything they didn't already know—about the case so maybe Kingsley would move on. And act as if he wanted a future with her. He was too obsessed with the past.

She scanned toward the left where she and her friends usually met. Dee and Marcy were already there and waved her over.

"It's two for one so we ordered you a pinot," Dee said as she hopped up to hug her. Marcy did the same and Gabi sat on one of the tall bar stools across from Marcy.

"Sounds perfect. Any word from Lena?" she asked as she took a sip of her wine. There was a fourth glass waiting for their other friend.

"She was stuck without a babysitter. Can you believe she has a kid? The girl who used to get locked out of the sorority house every dang night," Dee said.

"She's matured a lot."

"Having kids will do that to you, or so my mom says," Marcy said.

"It hasn't hurt you being around kids," Dee said. "But you really don't nanny that much anymore, do you?"

"No," Gabi said. She hadn't told her friends about Kingsley or the fact that she was living in at his place.

Lena arrived and regaled them with how fabulous her nine-month-old son was. Apparently he was above the curve on every chart, which made Gabi smile. She could hear the love in her friend's voice when she spoke about her little boy.

"Now that everyone is here," Gabi said. "I wanted to ask you about something that happened in college."

"Is it about how many men I've gotten from the tattoo you talked me into and then chickened out of getting yourself?" Dee asked.

"No. But you're welcome for that," Gabi said, smiling over at Dee. Dee worked for an interior-design company and had been responsible for the decor in Gabi's office.

"Then what is it?" Lena asked. "Is this the best wine ever, or is it just that I haven't been drinking lately?"

"It's a nice vintage," Marcy added. Her family had been vintners in California for more than 150 years and now Marcy worked in their marketing department. "Stop interrupting and let Gabi speak. Does it have anything to do with the fact that you are nannying for Kingsley Buchanan?"

"Yes," she said, looking at Marcy. "How did you know that?"

"I make it a habit to know what my friends are up to," Marcy said. "But go on."

"You're back with Kingsley?" Dee asked.

"It's complicated," Gabi said. She should have anticipated that they would know about her working for King.

"Explain it to us," Lena said. "Because we remember how he broke your heart."

"I know. You all were my rock back then."

"We still are," Dee said, putting her hand on Gabi's. The other women followed suit.

"Talk," Marcy said.

"Well, Kingsley asked me what I remembered about the night that Stacia died."

"Other than the fact that he slept with you and then went to her?"

"He didn't do that, Dee," Gabi said. "He wanted to know if I remembered any incidents of girls being slipped date-rape drugs at other parties. That's the angle they are working for what happened to Stacia."

"Sorry, Gabi. It just toasts my nuts that you waited so long to sleep with a guy and then—"

"My God punished me?" Gabi said.

Lena laughed and almost choked on her wine. "Out-of-wedlock sex… Has that been a continuing trend with you?"

"No, thank you very much. Do you guys remember anything?" Gabi asked.

"My roommate had something happen about three weeks before…Stacia," Lena said. "She was at a football party, I think. Joel was there with her and managed to get her home safe.

They both thought the drink was intended for someone else."

Joel had been one of the running backs on the football team, so Gabi made a mental note to mention it to Kingsley when she got back home.

"I can't remember anything, but to be honest I mainly just hung out with guys back then," Dee said.

Dee liked to have fun and thought life was all about sampling as much variety as she could. "Fair enough. Neither Hunter nor Kingsley remembers anything at the party after they started doing shots together. It was after he went back from my room."

"Really? I can't believe that. Hunter had a big fight with Stacia while you guys were gone, and when she came back, they got into it again."

"What?" Gabi asked. As far as she'd heard from Kingsley and Hunter, everything had been lovey-dovey between Stacia and Hunter. "They fought?"

"Yeah, I guess you would have missed it, and no one was really talking about it much after the arrest. But Hunter broke up with her earlier in the evening and she left."

Gabi didn't know what that meant other than either Kingsley had lied to her or Hunter had lied to him. "Who was she with when she came back?"

Dee looked at Marcy. "What was that guy's name? The one who always hung around you in the library? The sports-medicine guy."

"Garrett Keller," Marcy said. "Kind of a step down for Stacia."

"Definitely," Dee agreed. "That's when they had a second fight. Hunter took Stacia into the kitchen and all I heard was lots of yelling and then Kingsley went in there and dragged Hunter out. Stacia left a few minutes later."

"With the sports-medicine guy?" She'd never asked about any of this when she'd returned from Spain. By then, the charges had been dropped and Kingsley had moved on to the East Coast. She'd been trying to put it all behind her.

"No," Dee said. "He was talking with one of the players about an injury. I didn't see whom she left with. I thought she was on her own."

"That jives with what I remember," Lena said. "What about you, Marcy?"

"Yes, except I went home before any of that drama started. I had an exam to study for."

"Always hitting the books," Dee said.

The conversation drifted away from the past and into the present and Gabi tried to just relax and enjoy the evening with her friends. But she was worried.

It sounded as if Hunter hadn't been honest, and she really hoped he wasn't the reason why Kingsley's good name had been smeared.

When Gabi got back from drinks with her friends, Conner and Kingsley were playing games in the living room. It seemed like forever since she'd realized that he had come back to California to find closure to the past. She wanted to help him, especially after what she'd found out today, but it wasn't easy. Kingsley wasn't the kind of man who involved people in his business.

After putting Conner to bed and checking to make sure that Kingsley was in the media room watching the basketball game, she went into his office. The room was dark and not very welcoming as she entered it.

But that was probably just her imagination, since she knew she was sneaking where she shouldn't be. She went to his desk and using the flashlight on her phone started to look for anything that would give her a clue as to what he was looking for in the past.

Before she'd come home from meeting her friends, she'd gone to her own office and accessed the public records from Hunter and Kingsley's indictment.

It had been pretty cut-and-dried. She was surprised Hunter and Kingsley had been released, since there were at least a dozen witnesses who'd seen them with Stacia at the end of the evening. It hurt her a little to think Kingsley had gone back to the party after he left her, but that was in the past.

She was snooping around now trying to find something that would show her he had some evidence he wasn't sharing with her. Something that would help her put the pieces together after what she'd learned today from her friends. Was he hiding evidence to protect Hunter? Could there even be something here that implicated him? What the girls had told her had renewed her suspicions, though she had a lot of trouble believing he would actually kill Stacia.

The door opened; a shaft of light spilled into the room and a dark shadow filled the doorway.

"Should I drop to the floor and hide?"

"Uh, no. I'd prefer you tell me what you are doing in here," he said as he entered. He hit the light switch as he closed the door behind him and walked toward her.

He didn't appear mad, which she thought was a good thing. She knew she'd be pissed if she caught him going through her desk.

"Looking for answers. You said you didn't want to talk about it. I respect that, but I reread the indictment today and I figure you must have found something, that there must be some evidence of a smoking gun in here somewhere."

She fiddled with her phone, turning off the flashlight as Kingsley reached her. He leaned against his desk, sitting on the file she'd been about to open when he'd entered.

"I've found evidence of an intruder in my office." He pulled her between his legs and kept his hands on her hips.

He was trying to distract her with sex.

Dammit, it was working, too.

She wanted to let it go. It didn't affect her. But she cared for Kingsley and Conner. She wanted the stigma of that arrest and release to go away.

"But—"

He brought his mouth down on hers. He lifted her off her feet and changed their positions so that she was seated on the desk and he stood between her legs.

He pushed the skirt she was wearing up and reached between her legs to pull her panties down, drawing the fabric slowly down her legs and tossing it on the floor.

"Do you really want to talk about the past? When the future is so much more exciting," he said.

She didn't. She tangled her hands in the hair at the back of his neck and drew his head forward, shifting her body against his hand as their mouths met. She channeled all her questions into the kiss, all her dreams and desires. She thrust her tongue deep into his mouth, letting him know that she wasn't passive. Not where this was concerned.

Whatever he was doing, she wanted to help him. And she would, but right now she wanted him.

He tore his mouth from hers, kissed the length of her neck and slowly moved down her body, finding her nipple through the fabric of her dress and bra and scraping his teeth over it until it hardened. She fumbled between them trying to find his zipper and found his erection pressed against his pants.

She stroked him through his jeans as he sucked her nipple into his mouth. She undid his top button, carefully lowered the zipper of his pants and then pushed his underwear out of her way.

He was hot and hard, and she drew him closer to her with a light grasp on his body. She stroked her fingers up and down his length and then rubbed her finger over the tip, making small circles.

He looked up at her as he drew her hips toward the edge of the desk and positioned himself to enter her.

But he didn't move any farther; the tip of his body remained poised at the entrance of hers. She wanted to outwait him but she needed him, wanted to be filled with him now. She shifted and forced him inside her and he drew back his hips and returned with a forceful thrust that drove him deep inside her; she arched her back and grabbed his shoulders as shudders racked her body.

She felt pleasure so intense she couldn't breathe for a second as he drew back and thrust again. Their eyes met and their kiss deepened as he continued to rock in and out of her body until they both orgasmed and cried each other's names.

He drew her close to him, wrapped his big strong arms around her and held her as their breathing slowed.

"I'm here for revenge," he said softly. "To make the person who stole you from me pay."

His words were quietly whispered and she felt them all the way to her core. She didn't know what to say to that. So she just held on to him and pretended everything would be okay.

Fourteen

Gabi tried to sleep in Kingsley's arms in his big, comfortable king bed. But his words kept circling around in her head.

Vengeance.

Revenge.

These were things that she didn't believe in. They had a justice system for a reason, and so far she hadn't seen anything resolved by digging into the past. Nothing new had been uncovered on this vengeance mission. Kingsley needed to let go. He needed to move on.

Sure, she was the daughter of a judge. She'd always had faith in the judicial system. Heck, even Kingsley, who was innocent, had been let go. Why would he pursue revenge?

Because Conner could be hurt. It wasn't just about ignorant parents who wouldn't let him have a playdate. This was the kind of thing that would poison Kingsley. He thought he'd find something that everyone missed, but what if he didn't? Until he let it go they'd never be able to have the kind of future she knew she wanted with him.

She rolled away from him, staring at the clock on the nightstand. Time seemed to be moving so slowly.

She should have said something to him. Forced him to tell her what he really meant instead of allowing him to carry her back to bed to make love.

Love.

She'd been dancing around the word for days. Trying to figure out if she was just feeling the aftereffects of reuniting with her first love from college or if this was the real thing. She still wasn't sure. But she did know that a man who took justice into his own hands... She wouldn't allow herself to love a man like that.

"What's the matter?"

She rolled over and looked at him. In the dark room she could just make out his features. He was concerned. Rightly so: it was 3:05 in the morning. Most people were asleep.

"You said something earlier."

"I said a lot of things earlier."

He was being flip. She wished she could let this go. But then what? Would she just walk away and leave? The eighteen-year-old Gabi would have done that. But she wasn't that girl.

"Stop it. You know I want to talk about your quest for revenge."

"You know that I want to find the person who framed me and Hunter."

"I do. But finding him and getting revenge are two very different things," she said.

"I expect you to feel that way. Don't worry about my wrath. It won't hurt you."

How could he say that? "You don't really believe that, do you?"

"Yes."

"You're wrong."

"How do you figure? Once I have found the person I will alert the authorities and expose them for what they did."

That didn't sound so bad. "What exactly do you mean?"

"They lived free of the accusations and scrutiny that Hunter and I did. They have been walking around without any consequences while Stacia's murder has gone unsolved. I want justice for her. I will do whatever I have to that person. Once we find out who it is—"

"If you do that, Conner will live with the consequences," she said. "There's no way for you to do that and keep the source of the leak from the media."

"And I guess I'm supposed to just—what? What do you think would be the right choice? I'm happy to listen. But I am tired of living with the stigma of something I didn't do."

"Then let it go. Put it behind you."

"How can I?" he asked, rolling out of bed and striding over to his closet. He pulled on his robe and then turned to face her. "You had a small taste of what I put up with when the commissioners didn't want my money for the playground. But that's just part of it."

"I know. I'm sorry. But how will getting revenge help?"

"It will make me feel a hell of a lot better," Kingsley said.

But she doubted it. "Whoever it is..."

"We don't know yet. Chuck remembers seeing our coach at all of the parties where the women were drugged. And Hunter has been trying to talk to him but he's sick. Coach Gainer—he wouldn't have been drinking at the parties, so he would know something. He used to stop by to congratulate us when we won."

She put her head in her hands. This had been a mistake. Why couldn't she just have stayed quiet?

There was a chance that Kingsley wouldn't get his revenge at all, because finding out who had killed Stacia was proving harder than they'd ever anticipated. And she'd been looking for just a short time. He'd been doing this for years.

"Come back to bed," she said. "I'm sorry I started this tonight."

"I'm not. I know it's on your mind," he said. He stayed where he was.

"You have a point about the past. Maybe we should end this now. Before you are affected any more by it than you already have been."

She was tempted to say yes. To get out of his bed and walk out the door. It would be easier. But the truth was she'd been affected by that incident for her entire adult life. If Stacia hadn't been killed, and Kingsley hadn't been arrested, they would have dated and probably broken up. She would have graduated and gone to do something else. Without that incident, without that one night that had changed everything, her life would be different.

Not better.

Just different.

"I don't want to leave."

"Are you sure?"

There was something in his voice that warned her things were about to change.

"Yes."

He didn't move and she got out of bed and padded lightly over to him. In her heart she knew that she wanted to fix this, but was beginning to believe that she'd never be able to.

He had to let go if they were going to move on. She put her arms around him and rested her head against his chest. He stood there stiffly for another minute and then wrapped his arms around her. He rested his head on top of hers and she thought that this should feel more like coming home, but in her heart of hearts she knew the truth. This felt like goodbye.

Kingsley's dreams were troubled nightmares where he was left alone. He rolled to his side and jerked awake when he felt Gabi next to him.

Everything was unraveling out of his control and he knew it was only a matter of time before she left him. He couldn't see a future for them. In fact, he never had. Not really. Only now could he admit it.

He'd thought he'd come back to her for answers and to care for his son, but as he pulled her into his arms, he knew he'd come back to her for himself. Because he wanted to feel like the man he'd once been. A man who wasn't jaded by the life he'd lived.

But that man was gone.

And the only thing that came from holding on to Gabi would be to bring her down with him.

And he wasn't going to do that.

"King?" she asked in a sleepy voice.

"Yeah, baby?"

"Are you okay?" she asked.

No.

He was pretty sure he was never going to be okay again, but right now he didn't want to think about that. Instead he wanted to make love to Gabi one more time. To use a little bit of the California sunshine she'd brought into his life to illuminate the dark parts of his soul. Just one more time.

He kissed her. He wasn't shy about it, thrusting his tongue over her lips and teeth and then deep into her mouth. Her tongue slid against his and her arms came up to wrap around his shoulders.

He looked down into her eyes as he kissed her.

Their gazes met, and he realized she could read his intent.

She knew this was goodbye.

Tearing her mouth from his she started to speak, but he put his finger over her lips.

"No more talking tonight."

She nodded, her hands caressing his chest. Tracing over the tattoo of Conner's name. She leaned forward and kissed it. Traced the line of hair on his chest down past his belly button. She ran her finger around it and then pushed it into his belly button before going lower.

Wrapping her hand around his erection, she stroked him. He hardened even more as he reached for her breasts, cupped them and then rubbed his thumbs over her nipples.

She looked up at him again and he closed his eyes against the questions in hers. He rose up to his knees and tugged her up on her knees, as well. He turned her around so that her back was toward him and wrapped his arms around her. Held her pressed to him, burying his face in her neck as he rubbed his hands over her torso.

His erection nestled against her buttocks and

she undulated against him as he bit the nape of her neck. He felt her shiver in his arms as he reached between her legs and parted her intimate flesh.

He rubbed his finger over her clit in that swirling motion he knew she liked. Then he whispered dark, sexual words in her ear and heard her breath quicken. He leaned her forward, bracing her hands on the headboard as he pulled back, kissing his way down her back.

He took his time, biting gently as he moved down her spine. He kissed the small indentation right above her butt and then cupped the cheeks of her ass. He squeezed them and heard her moan in response.

Her legs parted and she looked back over her shoulder at him.

Her hair was wild and her eyes no longer held questions. Now he saw need and fire and demands there.

"Take me," she said.

Her words were like a hot glove brushing over his body. His blood felt heavier in his veins and his heartbeat pounded loudly in his ears.

He put his hands on her hips and shifted until he felt the opening of her body with the tip of his erection. He drew his hips back and slowly drove them forward until he was fully embedded in her.

He stayed there for a moment, reaching around to pluck at her nipples until she thrust her hips back against his, and then he slowly drew back before slamming forward again to fill her completely.

She arched her back and he continued thrusting into her until he felt that shiver of sensation down his spine and knew he was going to come.

He reached between her legs and flicked his finger over her. He drove harder and deeper into her until she arched frantically against him, her body tightening around his and driving him to his own climax. Her body continued to squeeze his, milking him of everything he had to give.

He wrapped his arm around her waist and put his hand between hers on the headboard to support himself as his breathing slowed. He rested his head in the middle of her back between her shoulder blades. He kissed her gently and then pulled her down onto the bed into his arms. He cradled her to him and rubbed his hand up and down her back until she drifted off to sleep.

He couldn't find sleep. Instead all he found were images of a future where he did the selfish thing and kept Gabi until her life slowly became sullied by his. He knew he had to let her go. And after all the things he'd walked away from, all the people he'd told himself he could live without, all the people who didn't matter, he realized she did. Walking away from her was the one thing he wasn't sure he was strong enough to do.

But he also realized he had no choice.

He'd meant it when he'd said he'd protect her. Even though he never realized he'd have to protect her from himself.

He got out of bed before dawn, showered and went down the hall to Conner's room. He got his son out of bed and dressed and then left a note for Gabi on her pillow in her room.

He got in his car and drove with no destination in mind. Conner was quiet in the backseat, not sure what was going on, and for once Kingsley knew he had no answers for his son. He only knew that he couldn't tell Gabi goodbye in person.

Gabi woke up alone in Kingsley's bed and knew before she got down to her own room and found the note on her pillow that he was gone. He'd said goodbye to her without words last night. She left the note on her pillow and went to take a shower.

He was letting her go. She had to be honest: she wasn't sure she was ready for that.

Hell, she thought as the hot water pounded down on her, she knew she wasn't ready. She'd spent the last month and a half falling in love with Kingsley. He was complicated and stubborn and way too fixated on the past, but she'd been confident she could change him.

Fix him.

Dammit.

She turned off the shower and toweled herself dry. She got dressed in a pair of linen pants and a long tunic shirt before blow-drying her hair. She took time with her makeup because focusing on that made her feel as though she was busy. But her mind just kept circling around and around.

He had rejected her again.

This time it hurt far worse, because she knew it was final. And she had loved him as a woman, not with the first crush of infatuation as she had before.

She took as long as she could in the bathroom and finally went to sit on her bed and opened up his note.

His handwriting was scrawling and masculine. She ran her fingers over it without really reading the words. Just putting off the inevitable a few moments longer.

Finally, she settled in and read.

Gabi,
Thank you for all you have done for Conner. You truly deserve all the accolades you've received from parenting blogs and magazines. But then I'm not surprised, since the woman I knew had a kind heart and a happy smile. I'm so glad to see you haven't lost those.

Our time together, as lovers, healed wounds

I didn't know I had from the past. I thought
that we had said everything we needed to that
day at the jail, but I realize now that we hadn't.

Saying goodbye is hard. Harder than anything I've done before, and so I took the coward's way out and put my words here in this
letter.

You were right when you said there was
no way to put aside the past and not have it
affect my future. And I see now there is no
way to protect you, either. Well, there is one
way, and I'm doing that now.

Please take good care of yourself and know
I wish you only the best.

Kingsley

That bastard.

He was leaving like this to avoid…what? Her?
The truth of the emotions between the two of
them?

She wouldn't let him do that. If he wanted to
dump her, he was going to have to do it to her
face. None of this leaving a note.

She grabbed her purse and walked through

the house, finding Mrs. Tillman in the kitchen drinking coffee and playing that game on her phone she loved.

"Have you seen Kingsley?"

"No. He was gone when I arrived," Mrs. Tillman said.

"I'm going out, but I will be back later. When he comes back, would you mind asking him to call me?"

"Not at all, Gabi," Mrs. Tillman said.

She got out to her car and dialed Hunter's number and got his voice mail. "It's Gabi. I'm looking for Kingsley. Can you call me?"

Then she drove to her office in Carmel. Abby was sitting at Melissa's old desk and smiled when Gabi walked in. Melissa had moved into an office now that she was assistant manager. Gabi went down the hall to her own office and pretended that it was a normal day. She wrote her column. But she was distracted. Where was he?

Did he really just think she would walk away without talking to him?

Her intercom buzzed.

"Yes, Abby?"

"Mr. Ortiz and Mrs. O'Malley are here to see you."

The county commissioners? She was surprised. Though she had expected a response to the email she'd sent them.

"Send them down."

A moment later her door opened and she stood to greet her visitors.

"Hello. What can I do for you today?" Gabi asked, gesturing for them to take a seat in the guest chairs in front of her desk.

"We thought coming to see you might be better than sending an email," Mr. Ortiz said. "I wanted to apologize for the way the meeting went."

"Me, as well," Mrs. O'Malley said. "We've had time to discuss Mr. Buchanan and his generous contribution to our city in some detail after we received your email. The committee feels we might have been too hasty in our judgment."

Gabi crossed her hands together. "I'm glad to hear that. What changed your minds?"

"It was something you said in your email, that

we all must let our actions speak to the type of person we are. Mr. Buchanan has never had another incident like the one in college, and when we pulled up his charity work, well, we were embarrassed by the way the committee reacted," Mr. Ortiz said. "If you and Mr. Buchanan are still interested, we'd love to go forward with building the playground, and we'd even like to name it in his honor."

Gabi swallowed hard against the emotions welling up inside her. This was the kind of gesture that Kingsley needed to see.

"I will discuss it with him and let you know later this week. But I'm sure he will be happy to move ahead with the project," Gabi said.

She showed the commissioners out and texted Kingsley that they needed to talk.

He texted back that he'd said all that needed saying.

And she clenched her jaw and sent him one more message that she deserved the chance to say goodbye to Conner in person.

Kingsley simply responded that they'd drop by her office later in the day. She wondered what he was going to do? Had he just left the house to avoid a messy goodbye or was he leaving the West Coast permanently?

She wasn't pleased with the way he acted. But at least she'd have the chance to see him again and maybe make him admit that he cared for her. The committee had changed their minds; perhaps time was all that was needed to heal the wounds of the past. Or at least she hoped it was.

Fifteen

Kingsley pulled into the parking lot of Gabi's office and sat there for a long minute. He'd taken Conner to the Redwood Forest and his son was worn out from walking and talking. His lie that Gabi had a full day of meetings had worked on his son.

Conner couldn't wait to tell her about everything they'd done and it made Kingsley a little sad that Gabi would no longer be a part of his life. But they were fine before she'd become part of their family and they would be fine again.

He knew what was required to keep Gabi safe and also, if he were being honest, to protect the two of them. There were no guarantees that they'd ever put the past to rest. What if she stayed in his life and then one day had enough of it? Better to end things now.

He got Conner out of his car seat and took his hand as they walked to the office building.

Abby was seated behind the desk talking to Melissa when they walked in.

"Hey," Conner said.

"Hello, kiddo," Melissa said.

"We're here to see Gabi," Kingsley said.

"She asked to see you alone first," Melissa said. "I have a new book on knights if you want to read it, Conner."

"Daddy?"

"It's okay, buddy. I'll be right back," Kingsley said.

He didn't want to be alone with Gabi. He wasn't sure he trusted himself with her. He wanted her, but this thing between them had grown way past young lust. He wasn't sure it had ever been just about lust.

He knocked on her door.

"Come in."

He took a deep breath before he opened the door. He had chosen his path and nothing—not even Gabi—could shake him from it.

He walked into her office and closed the door behind him. She looked much the same as she had the first time he'd come to see her here. Very poised and professional, sitting behind her desk and watching him with a guarded expression in her dark chocolate eyes.

"What's up?" he asked.

"Are you kidding me right now?" she asked. Her words revealed that the serenity she projected was only on the surface. Something deeper simmered underneath and he had the very real feeling that he wasn't getting out of her office without a few burn marks.

It was okay. He could handle it.

"No, I'm not. I thought my letter said everything that needed saying."

"Well, it didn't. I didn't get a chance to tell you how I felt," she said.

"Is that necessary?" he asked. "I think we both know there is no way of moving forward."

"No way? What happened? Was it what I said

last night? Because I'm not going to apologize for that. I mean, I know it was the middle of the night when doubts are strongest, but in the clear light of day—"

"I realized that you were right. Doubts aren't just clearest in the middle of the night, Gabi, they are also revealed to be the truth. You were right when you said I'd never be free of the repercussions of revenge, but you didn't mention the other item. The past. I'm never going to be free of it."

"That's not true," she said, getting up and coming around her desk. "Today the county commissioners stopped by and apologized. They are honored to have you sponsor the park."

"That's nice. But I'm sure it was financially motivated and it changes nothing. People are always going to remember the headline arrest and the truth—whatever it is—will hold no sway over them."

Gabi reached for him but he stepped away. He wasn't sure he could handle her touching him right now.

"Really? Is that the way things are between us now?"

He looked into those eyes, the same ones he'd avoided last night, and knew that he didn't want it to be over. He wanted to find a way to have her and keep her and protect her. To create the family he'd been searching for with her. The family he wanted for Conner and for himself, too.

"Yes."

"Bastard."

He nodded. Better to end it now and like this. So he'd never be tempted to come back and try again. "I'll bring Conner in to say goodbye."

"If that's what you must do. I'm not sure why you are cutting me out of your life. I thought this time we were being honest with each other and building something real."

"I don't know how I lied."

"When you invited me to have dinner with you and we walked on the beach. You seduced me with romance and I let you because…well, it doesn't matter. Why did you do that? Was it just a game to you?"

"No. It was never a game," he said.

"Then why?"

"The reason no longer matters," he said.

"Figures you'd say that," she said.

"What do you mean by that?"

"Just that you've been covering up for Hunter, so I guess I should never expect the truth from you about anything."

"I haven't lied to you," he said. "What the hell are you talking about with Hunter?"

"He and Stacia broke up the night she died. I find it hard to believe you didn't know that."

"I didn't."

"Well, maybe you should be cutting the people who have hurt you from your life instead of the ones who are just trying to help you," Gabi said.

"How were you trying to help me?" he asked. He'd figure out the Hunter thing later.

"By loving you, Kingsley. But a man like you is too hard, too locked away in the past to let something like love lead you out of it. And frankly, I'm tired of trying."

She walked out of the office and down the hall to Conner. She hugged him and told him she had to start working for another family. And the smooth, professional way she handled it made Kingsley realize she'd said goodbye to children before.

He wondered if she even cared for his son, but when she stood up and turned her head he saw the tears glistening in her eyes and realized that she did.

He wondered if he'd made a mistake. She was making him question things he'd always thought were true, but it was too late to go back.

Kingsley was angry. Gabi's arguments made a certain kind of sense, but surely Hunter hadn't been lying to him the entire time. He texted Hunter to come over to his place, and they met there twenty minutes later.

He looked haggard. His friend wasn't dealing with being back in California well at all. His family had never really believed in his innocence and Kingsley didn't want to heap onto him the same accusations as they had.

But there were questions that needed answering. And he needed those answers now.

"What's up? Did Gabi find out anything useful?" Hunter asked. He walked straight to the sideboard and poured himself two fingers of scotch. He downed it in one gulp before turning to face him.

Kingsley couldn't speak for a second. This was a man he thought he knew better than anyone… Did he really know any person at all?

"She did. She found several witnesses who saw you and Stacia fighting the night she died."

Hunter cursed and poured himself some more scotch. "Okay. So now what?"

"Is it true?"

"Yes."

"Why haven't you ever said anything about that?"

Hunter put the glass down and shoved his hands through his thick blond hair. He stared at the floor for a long moment and then looked up. His gray eyes were dark and there was something in his gaze that Kingsley had seen only one time before—when they'd both been locked up in the holding cell.

"I was afraid you'd think I was guilty," he said at last.

Kingsley walked over to his friend and clapped him on the shoulder. "You know that you're not."

Hunter didn't say anything and Kingsley dropped his hand. "You do know that, right?"

"I don't. I mean, the entire night is hazy. I've never been violent. You know I can't even go hunting or anything. But I've never really been able to remember what happened. And it's only been by searching for the truth that I hope I will find it."

Damn.

This sucked. Majorly sucked. He'd been on this path believing they were wrongly accused. He'd been prepared to ruin another man's life because of Hunter. Because he believed that they were both innocent.

"Why the hell haven't you said anything before this?" Kingsley asked.

"You were the only one who had faith in me. You're the only person in the world who looks at me like I'm a man and not a monster, King. I couldn't give that up."

He got it. He knew what it felt like to have

the entire world staring at him as if he were a monster.

"What do you remember?"

He needed to get to the bottom of what Hunter had done that night. Maybe if they were able to match it up with what the other witnesses saw... they could both be satisfied that Hunter wasn't guilty.

Hunter walked over to the French doors that led to the patio. The patio where Kingsley had that first date with Gabi. That night had changed things for him. Made him believe that once he finished this investigation he could move on— have a future. But the things she'd said tonight... well, maybe that wasn't truly in the cards for them.

"I have been over it a million times," Hunter said.

"Not with me. So we were both at the party, drinking, dancing—I left with Gabi. What happened while I was gone?" Kingsley asked.

"Stacia and I went up to my room to be alone. Things were so intense between us and I knew things would change once I was in the pros, so

I wanted to cool it down…but I couldn't. She was… She was in my blood, King. I mean, I told her I thought we should cool it down, but she thought I was joking. And for a second I let her believe that but I knew I wanted to enjoy being young and a football god so I had to break it off with her."

"Football god?" Kingsley asked.

"Yeah. You know how cocky I was back then. Anyway, we fought. She got mad and said she didn't need me and left. I stayed in my room for—I don't know, maybe twenty minutes, and then Chuck came up and dragged me back to the party."

"I got back about then," Kingsley said. "You and Chuck were at the keg, right?"

"Yes. But I wasn't in the mood to drink," Hunter said.

"Beer. You weren't in the mood to drink beer, but we both started doing shots."

"Yes. When Stacia came back in, she was with all those guys. I didn't like it, but knew I couldn't stop her."

Things were starting to become clearer for

Kingsley. They'd been doing shots when Chuck got up and left. Then someone had brought over the next round... Kingsley searched his mind, but it was hazy. He'd been conflicted over Gabi. But it was beginning to come back to him, how Hunter had been pouring his heart out once they'd gotten a little bit drunk. How Kingsley had been consoling him.

"I remember now. You were telling me that you loved her but she was better off without you. That you weren't ready to be tied down."

Hunter looked up. "I said that?"

"Yeah."

"Damn. Then I didn't kill her, did I?" Hunter asked. "I mean, we were too drunk to do anything."

"We were. Remember I spilled the bottle of Jägermeister and someone brought us another one...I can't remember who, do you?"

Hunter tipped his head back, staring up at the ceiling, and then shook his head. "No. Did Gabi get anything else from the witnesses?"

"Just that most people were too drunk to remember much and one girl—Amber Riley—was passed out in the corner," Kingsley said.

"Coach," Kingsley said. "He came in at the end, didn't he? Warned us to get out before the cops came."

"Yeah. I remember that. I didn't see Stacia again," Hunter said.

"Did you get to talk to him?"

"No. He's still in the hospital, but one of the nurses told me he's going home. That's why I'm back. I'm going over to see him tomorrow."

"Maybe then we can find out what happened. But one thing is for sure," Kingsley said. "You didn't kill Stacia, Hunter. Don't torture yourself with that for a moment longer. We were together and with Coach."

Hunter nodded. "I wish…"

"We both do."

He clapped his friend on the back. A few minutes later Hunter went to the guest room that Kingsley kept for him and Kingsley went into Conner's room. He stood over his son and remembered all the reasons why he was here. Why he had decided to stop running.

It didn't matter that he had screwed things up more than once. He always—always—made them right. And he knew that he was going to have to figure out how to get Gabi back. He needed her.

Gabi had contacted Mrs. Tillman to find out when Conner and Kingsley would both be out of the house. And then she and Melissa had gone over to pack up her stuff. Conner, she suspected with Mrs. Tillman's help, had left her a printout of the photo of the three of them dressed up for their Aladdin adventure. She should have realized then that saying goodbye was going to be hard.

She had warned all the nannies who worked for her not to get too attached, because nannies weren't part of the family, but she'd forgotten that rule and now she was paying for it.

"That's the last of the office stuff. I'm going to head back unless you need me for anything else," Melissa said.

"No, that's okay. I'll probably go home from here, so I'll see you tomorrow," Gabi said.

Melissa gave her a sympathetic smile before turning to leave. She finished packing up her closet and the bathroom things she'd left behind. She had been so sure that she'd outmaneuver Kingsley and force him to realize that they were meant to be together.

But she should have remembered he was very good at getting his way.

She was zipping her suitcase closed when she heard music coming from down the hall. It was an old Matchbox Twenty song, "If You're Gone." She followed the sound of Rob Thomas's voice to the open patio door, where she found Conner dressed like Aladdin waiting for her.

"Princess," he said formally. "We have been waiting for you. Come with me."

"Conner, I don't think this is a good idea. Your daddy and I—"

"Please, Gammi," Conner said. "Please."

She nodded and slipped her hand into his. He led her to the garden area, where a brass lamp waited on a table.

"That's for you," Conner said.

She looked around, having expected to see

Kingsley here somewhere. "Thank you. I will put it on my desk so I can see it every day."

"No. You have to rub the lamp," Conner said.

She looked at him standing there watching her with anticipation, a serious expression on his face.

She knelt down next to him. "Should we both do it?"

"Just you," Conner said.

She rubbed the lamp and was surprised when smoke started to rise from it. Just a small burst. She looked at Conner, but he was staring over her shoulder. She turned around and saw Kingsley standing there.

He was dressed only in a pair of loose linen trousers and had his hands on his hips. He had two big brass bracelets on each wrist.

"What is your wish, mistress?" he asked.

"Uh, I'm not sure what's going on," she admitted.

"You've uncovered the magic genie of the lamp," Conner said. "You get three wishes."

Her heart was beating so loudly she thought that everyone could hear it. She wasn't sure what this was all about but had the feeling that Kingsley wasn't saying goodbye.

"What should I wish for?" she asked Conner.

"I'd ask for you to be in my family," he said. "We miss you, Gammi."

"Is that true, Kingsley?" Gabi asked.

"Yes, it is. I'm sorry for everything that happened. I wanted to protect you and thought... well, I thought you'd be better off without me, but my life is dull without you. I want you back."

"Me, too," Conner said.

She hugged Conner and got to her feet to walk over to Kingsley. "Why the genie outfit? I don't want magic tricks. I want the real man."

"I know that," Kingsley said. "But the truth is I love you and I will do whatever I have to in order to make you feel the same way."

"I love you, too, Kingsley, but that was never the issue. Can you let me be a part of your life? Trust me to stay by your side?"

"I can. In fact, that's why I'm your genie. I'll be by your side granting all of your wishes."

"And if I wish for you to give up on this revenge idea?" she asked.

"Then I will continue to help Hunter—we have to talk about that later—but will not be involved in taking justice into my own hands," Kingsley said.

She looked into his eyes, searching for the truth, and it was there for her to see. He wasn't hiding from her or from his emotions anymore. He loved her.

She couldn't believe it. It was what she'd wanted from the first time they met. A school-girl's crush had developed into a true and deep love. She hadn't dared to hope. Had thought he was too caught in the past to ever make a real commitment to her, but she was glad to be proved wrong.

She threw herself into his arms and he caught her and swung her around in a circle, kissing her.

"You've made all my wishes come true," she said.

"As you've done for me. Wishes I never dared to dream I could have," Kingsley said.

"If Gammi isn't going to use all her wishes, can I have one?" Conner asked.

Kingsley started laughing and Gabi reached for Conner's hand.

"What do you want?" Kingsley asked, striking his genie pose again with his hands on his hips.

"A family. The three of us to be a family," he said.

"I want that, too," Kingsley said. "Will you marry me, Gabi?"

She looked at these two men who meant the world to her and realized that she hadn't dreamed she could ever be as happy as she was in this moment.

"Yes, I will marry you."

"Yay!" Conner yelled, dancing around them.

Kingsley drew her into his arms and kissed her. She put her hands on his face and looked into his eyes, remembering the first time she met him and fell for him. She'd thought she'd found her true love and now she realized that the love she had for Kingsley was deeper and stronger than ever before.

He dropped to one knee and pulled a ring from his pocket.

"What are you doing, Daddy?"

"Asking Gabi to marry me," Kingsley said to Conner.

Conner came over and knelt next to his dad and Gabi felt as if her heart couldn't get any fuller. Kingsley reached for her hand and when she gave it to him, Conner reached up and held it too.

"Will you marry me, Gabi? Will you be a part of our family?"

"Will you, Gammi?" Conner added.

She knelt down in front of the Buchanan men and wrapped her arms around them both. "Yes, I will."

Kingsley drew back and took a ring box from his pocket. He opened it up and Conner put his hand on his dad's arm and lifted the ring out. He held it out to Gabi and King helped Conner put it on her finger.

They spent the rest of the day together, and when Conner was safely tucked in bed for the night, Kingsley made love to her. He held her close all night long and promised her she'd spent the rest of her life by his side.

* * * * *

MILLS & BOON®

Why shop at millsandboon.co.uk?

Each year, thousands of romance readers find their perfect read at millsandboon.co.uk. That's because we're passionate about bringing you the very best romantic fiction. Here are some of the advantages of shopping at www.millsandboon.co.uk:

* **Get new books first**—you'll be able to buy your favourite books one month before they hit the shops

* **Get exclusive discounts**—you'll also be able to buy our specially created monthly collections, with up to 50% off the RRP

* **Find your favourite authors**—latest news, interviews and new releases for all your favourite authors and series on our website, plus ideas for what to try next

* **Join in**—once you've bought your favourite books, don't forget to register with us to rate, review and join in the discussions

Visit **www.millsandboon.co.uk**
for all this and more today!